Praise for Dixie Browning

"There is no one writing romance today
who touches the heart and tickles the ribs like
Dixie Browning. The people in her books are as
warm and real as a sunbeam and just as lovely."
—*New York Times* bestselling author Nora Roberts

"Dixie Browning has given the romance industry
years of love and laughter in her wonderful books."
—*New York Times* bestselling author Linda Howard

"A true pioneer in romantic fiction,
the delightful Dixie Browning is a reader's
most precious treasure, a constant source
of outstanding entertainment."
—*Romantic Times Magazine*

"Each of Dixie's books is a keeper guaranteed
to warm the heart and delight the senses."
—*New York Times* bestselling author
Jayne Ann Krentz

"Dixie's books never disappoint—
they always lift your spirit!"
—*USA Today* bestselling author Mary Lynn Baxter

Dear Reader,

Welcome to Silhouette Desire, where every month you can count on finding six passionate, powerful and provocative romances.

The fabulous Dixie Browning brings us November's MAN OF THE MONTH, *Rocky and the Senator's Daughter,* in which a heroine on the verge of scandal arouses the protective *and* sensual instincts of a man who knew her as a teenager. Then Leanne Banks launches her exciting Desire miniseries, THE ROYAL DUMONTS, with *Royal Dad,* the timeless story of a prince who falls in love with his son's American tutor.

The Bachelorette, Kate Little's lively contribution to our 20 AMBER COURT miniseries, features a wealthy businessman who buys a date with a "plain Jane" at a charity auction. The intriguing miniseries SECRETS! continues with *Sinclair's Surprise Baby,* Barbara McCauley's tale of a rugged bachelor with amnesia who's stunned to learn he's the father of a love child.

In *Luke's Promise* by Eileen Wilks, we meet the second TALL, DARK & ELIGIBLE brother, a gorgeous rancher who tries to respect his wife-of-convenience's virtue, while *she* looks to *him* for lessons in lovemaking! And, finally, in Gail Dayton's delightful *Hide-and-Sheikh,* a lovely security specialist and a sexy sheikh play a game in which both lose their hearts…and win a future together.

So treat yourself to all six of these not-to-be-missed stories. You deserve the pleasure!

Enjoy,

Joan Marlow Golan

Joan Marlow Golan
Senior Editor, Silhouette Desire

Please address questions and book requests to:
Silhouette Reader Service
U.S.: 3010 Walden Ave., P.O. Box 1325, Buffalo, NY 14269
Canadian: P.O. Box 609, Fort Erie, Ont. L2A 5X3

Rocky and the Senator's Daughter

DIXIE BROWNING

Published by Silhouette Books
America's Publisher of Contemporary Romance

SILHOUETTE BOOKS

RECYCLED PAPER

ISBN 0-373-76399-9

ROCKY AND THE SENATOR'S DAUGHTER

Copyright © 2001 by Dixie Browning

Visit Silhouette at www.eHarlequin.com

Printed in U.S.A.

DIXIE BROWNING

is an award-winning painter and writer, mother and grandmother. Her father was a big-league baseball player, her grandfather a sea captain. In addition to her nearly 80 contemporary romances, Dixie and her sister, Mary Williams, have written more than a dozen historical romances under the name Bronwyn Williams. Contact Dixie at www.dixiebrowning.com or at P.O. Box 1389, Buxton, NC 27920.

One

The suite was small, the acoustics brutal. The guests were a mixture of media types, politicians, wives and significant others. All were talking at once; few, if any, were listening. At least there was no band to overcome. The noise level had hit him when he'd first stepped off the elevator. Considering that until recently, as an accredited journalist, Rocky had covered nearly every noisy, crowded hotspot on the globe, it shouldn't have been a problem.

It was. He wanted out.

From across the room he watched as the honoree edged past two network anchors, who appeared to be comparing pinky rings, and absently handed his glass to a well-known syndicated sportswriter.

Rocky waited. He had come to help honor his old bureau chief. So far he hadn't managed to get close enough to pay his respects.

"Not leaving yet, are you?"

Dan Sturdivant, retiring bureau chief at Graves Worldwide, had trained a surprising number of the reporters in the business today, including Rocky. Now pushing seventy-five, he had a heart condition, ulcers and essential tremors. Which was the sole reason Rocky, even though he hadn't worked with the man in years, had given up his quiet Sunday evening for this bash at the Shoreham. He'd been a hungry young idealist fresh out of college when Dan had taken him in, sifted through his headful of useless garbage, refilling his brain with a few basic tenets, and set him to work covering court news.

Welcome to the real world. Everything he had gone on to achieve, Rocky owed to this man.

"Heard you'd quit the business," the old man said by way of greeting.

"News travels fast." It was a standing joke between them. "Call it a sabbatical."

"Skip the euphemisms. You're too young to quit."

"I'm tired, Dan."

"You and me both, son, but tired won't cut it. You gotta have a better excuse than that."

He had one. And, yeah, tired would do it when a man had been carrying a load of heartbreak for eight years. Dan knew the story, but it wasn't something either man had ever discussed.

"Stick around, this bash can't last forever. God, what did I ever do to deserve this kind of punishment?" He shook his shiny bald head and tried to look as if he weren't loving every minute of it.

"Braves game. If I leave now I can probably make it home by the third."

"Mets'll take 'em, you don't want to watch the slaughter."

"In your dreams."

"You know where I live if you want to talk."

Rocky nodded. Dan nodded. Message sent and received.

He wasn't ready to talk about what he was going to do with the rest of his life. Financially he had to do something, but he didn't have to decide yet—not for a few more weeks. Or months. Maybe if he got hungry enough, he could find the motivation to try a weekly column. Two different syndicates had put out feelers.

But first he had to get over Julie. His marriage had ended in the summer of ninety-four, when a drunk driver had rammed head-on into the car his wife had been driving home from the library, breaking her back and causing irreparable damage to her head. He had buried her six months ago. He hadn't cried then. More than seven years of watching her lying there, alive and yet not alive—Julie and yet not Julie—had used up his lifetime quota of tears.

For seven years he'd taken her bouquets of her favorite flower. Flowers she couldn't see, couldn't smell, but he told himself that deep down, she sensed they were there. And that he loved her—would always love her, no matter what. Finally in early February, on a cold, rainy morning, he had buried her beside her parents, after a private memorial service. Then he'd gone home alone and deliberately drunk himself insensible.

A week later he had handed in his resignation, poured three bottles of double-malt whisky down the sink and stocked up on colas. He'd spent the summer brooding, watching baseball and rereading *War and*

Peace. Once the baseball season ended, he'd promised himself, he would start thinking about what he was going to do with the rest of his life.

It had taken Dan's retirement party to pry him out of his apartment and back into circulation. About time, he acknowledged with bitter amusement. His social skills, never particularly impressive, had grown dull with lack of use.

"Mac, glad to see you." Quietly, he greeted a guy who had once covered the White House for one of the major networks, then edged past him.

"Hey, Rock—where you been? Haven't seen you around lately."

"Rocko, good to see you, man," someone else called out.

He made it about halfway to the door, weaving his way through clusters of people he knew vaguely. Got held up between one of the massive sofas and a cluster of women picking over the bones of some poor devil obviously known to them all.

"Did you see him at that last press conference? I swear, if I looked like that, I'd slit my—"

A redhead wearing a black suit about two sizes too small leaned forward, sloshing her drink dangerously close to the rim of her glass, and said in a whisky-thickened voice, "Honey, I peeked into his underwear drawer, and believe you me, those rumors are the gospel truth!"

Gossip was the order of the day. Snide comments, catty remarks. Rocky glanced at his watch. He'd planned on being in and out within twenty minutes, tops. It had taken him that long just to work his way across the room. Anyone who had been around pols and media types as long as he had should have known what to expect. With scandal in D.C. as plentiful as cherry blossoms in spring, it didn't take much effort to pick up a thread here and another one there and weave them into a story that could ruin a few lives and leapfrog a career.

Thank God he hadn't chosen that route. He didn't have the stomach for it. Once he'd realized that his objectivity as a reporter was beginning to give way to advocacy, he had asked for reassignment. It had meant not seeing as much of Julie, but then, the hours spent by her bedside had been more for his sake than for hers. The doctor had told him right from the first that, while she might appear to be responding, critical portions of her brain had been injured. That it was only a matter of time before her vital functions began to shut down.

Despite the prognosis, he had gone on hoping. Reading to her, taking her flowers, relating news about people they both knew. Resignation had set in slowly, over a matter of years. He wasn't even aware of when he'd stopped hoping.

Someone bumped into him, spilling a drink on his sleeve.

"Oops, sorry."

"No problem." He had to get out of here. This time he almost made it to the door. "Excuse me—pardon me."

The woman blocking his exit turned. Her eyes widened as she gave him a slow once-over. "Well, hello, honey. Not leaving so soon, are you?"

"Another appointment." No thanks. It's been a long, dry spell, but I'm not that hard up.

Three women emerged from one of the suite's two bathrooms and paused, still talking, blocking the door to the hallway. A brunette with a spectacular super-structure was saying, "Well, anyhow, like I said, the first two publishers turned it down flat. They as good as told us to take it to the tabloids, but the very next day my agent showed it to another publisher and he offered us a six-figure advance, and my agent said—"

"Forget what your agent said, Binky, check with a lawyer. He's the one you want beside you the first time you're sued for libel."

"No chance. Who's going to step forward and claim credit for something like that? Besides, my agent says I'm safe because this is a first-person account and I'm not actually naming names."

"Aw, come on, Binky, you're not claiming to be Sully's first, are you?"

All three women laughed. "Are you kidding?"

Amused in spite of himself Rocky squeezed past and waited for the elevator. The woman called Binky was still holding forth. If he wasn't mistaken, she did a social column for one of the weeklies. He'd once heard her chest referred to as the Grand Tetons.

"Listen, I'm talking group stuff here," she said, her heavily made-up eyes sparkling avidly. "Kinky like you wouldn't believe! Poor Sully said his wife was about as exciting as wet bread. He had a taste for fancier fare, if you know what I mean."

"I met her once at a fund-raiser. His wife, I mean. She struck me as real uptight. All the same, I'd watch my back if I were you. You know what they say about those quiet types."

Rocky would take his chances with a quiet type

anyday over these pampered piranhas. He felt sorry for the wife of whatever poor jerk they were discussing. Evidently she'd been victimized first by her husband and now was about to be pilloried all over again by the public's insatiable appetite for dirt.

"Yeah, well who's interested in her?" Binky unbuttoned her black jacket to reveal the scrap of ecru lace she wore instead of a blouse. "Did I tell you they're rushing production? They've got three editors working on it, and marketing has booked me on all the talk shows. I mean, with a title like *The Senator's Daughter's Husband's Other Women,* it's gonna make all the lists, probably the top slot, because my agent says—"

The elevator stopped. The doors opened. Rocky stood there, frowning in thought until the doors silently closed again. He had once known a senator's daughter who had later married a congressman. Was she talking about *that* particular senator's daughter? The one who had married *that* particular congressman? Even by Washington standards, that had been rough. The press had been all over it.

Not that he'd really known her, Rocky amended as another elevator stopped to let off a couple of late arrivals. Still frowning, he stepped onboard. Actually, he'd only spoken to her one time, years before her father's misdeeds had begun to surface. Years before she had married the senator's trained seal in the House—a man who had gone down in flames in a separate scandal shortly after the senator had been figuratively tarred and feathered and ridden out of town on a rail.

Rocky had been covering the Middle East Summit

when the wedding had taken place. He remembered watching some of the coverage. The Sullivans and Joneses, while hardly in the Kennedy class, had still made a pretty big splash. Even the veep had attended the festivities. She'd made a beautiful bride. Not pretty in the usual sense, but with an innate poise that could easily be called regal. He'd caught a flash of that funny little half smile he remembered from their one and only meeting years earlier.

It had been a few years after that when the lid had blown off the first scandal. There'd been rumblings before, but nothing that couldn't be blamed on partisan politics. Finally, with its back to the wall, Justice had appointed an independent council to investigate, and Rocky had watched from whatever assignment he happened to be on as one after another, Senator J. Abernathy Jones's sins were laid bare.

The feeding frenzy had eventually brought down half a dozen smaller fry, but if memory served, the young congressman his daughter had married some six years earlier had not been among them. Sullivan's downfall had come a year or so later, following what had started out as a simple drug bust. By then the senator had been history.

Rocky hadn't wanted to watch the second chapter unfold, but with all the networks covering the story, it was unavoidable. And, unfortunately, understandable. Juicy scandals had a way of selling newspapers, hiking ratings, making careers. That had been proven too many times to be in doubt.

So he'd witnessed the handsome young congressman's downfall, watched as the press—his own peers—had hounded the man's wife, his office staff, even his barber. He remembered thinking once, seeing Sullivan's wife trapped by a mob of yelling reporters between the front door of her Arlington house and a car driven by her housekeeper, that Joan of Arc might have worn the same stoic expression.

That had been more than a year ago. Immersed in his own crisis, Rocky hadn't thought of her since then.

Now he did.

Her name had been Sarah Mariah Jones the first time he'd ever seen her. It had been at a fund-raiser sponsored by a couple of Hollywood celebrities. She must have been about fifteen years old at the time. He'd been a green reporter and she'd been a gawky kid trying hard to look as if she weren't dying to be someplace else. *Anyplace* else. He remembered reading somewhere that her mother had died recently. The senator's habit of using her for photo ops, then shoving her into the background had been pretty well established. Rumor had it that years ago he had forgotten and left her at a town hall meeting in a school gymnasium for about six hours before he'd remembered to send someone to pick her up.

It had occurred to him that day at the fund-raiser that she'd been painfully aware of her own role in her father's struggling reelection campaign. She was there to be used the way he used everyone else, then shoved aside until the need arose again. The old pol had played the family card for all it was worth, ever since his opponent, a married man with three children, had been caught in a compromising situation with an aide.

It had been the standard celebrity bash. Only those journalists who shared the senator's ideology had been invited to meet and mingle with the glitterati. Rocky, who had considered himself politically unbiased at that early stage of his budding career, had been on his way out when he'd spotted the girl.

In a dress that was obviously expensive and painfully unflattering, the young Sarah Mariah had watched her father buttonhole another major contributor, clasp his hand, slap him on the arm and then proceed to apply the thumbscrews. Something about her expression had caught his attention. It reminded him too much of children he'd seen with eyes far too old for their tender years.

Which was probably why, from a mixture of boredom and sympathy, he had collected a cup of tea and a finger sandwich—asparagus and cream cheese, he remembered distinctly—and made his way over to the potted palm where she'd gone to earth.

"Hi. My name's Rocky and I'm a truant officer. Do you have your parents' permission to be here?" Silly stuff, but hell—she was just a kid.

"How do you do, Mr. Rocky. My name is Anonymous Jones, and if you blow my cover I'll be deported at the very least, beheaded if the king's having a bad hair day."

"Yeah, I figured as much." They'd both stared at the senator's trademark silver pompadour. "Brought you a last meal just in case. Asparagus sandwiches. They looked like a safer bet than those small brown things."

"The barbecued loin of weasel?"

"Those were all gone. There were a couple of the guppy filets left, but you know what they say about seafood."

"No, what do they say?"

He'd shrugged. "Beats me."

She had smiled then. A quick, spontaneous smile that was gone almost before it appeared. They had talked for a few minutes and then she'd reached for the tea. Her hand had struck the saucer, and in trying to catch the cup before it spilled, she'd managed to dump the sandwich onto his shoes. Cream-cheese side down. Smack on the laces, where it couldn't easily be wiped off.

The poor kid had looked stricken, so he'd forgotten his own irritation and made some crack about asparagus being a known insect repellant. "It's the scent, you know? You ever sniff an asparagus? Whoa. Really bad stuff."

She'd looked so grateful he'd been afraid she was going to do something gauche, like kissing his hand. Mumbling something about an appointment, he'd left before she could embarrass them both.

Even then it had occurred to him that she had vulnerable eyes. Far too vulnerable, considering the circles she moved in. He remembered thinking that with a crook like J. Abernathy Jones for a father, she'd be in therapy before the year was out, if she wasn't already.

Sarah Mariah Jones Sullivan, he mused now. Daughter of Senator J. Abernathy Jones, who had been reelected by the skin of his teeth shortly after their one and only meeting.

Wife—make that widow—of Junior Congressman Stanley Sullivan, the senator's protégé and hand-picked puppet. Despite his reputation as a latter-day John Kennedy, the jerk had been nothing more than a dirty, womanizing lightweight who had barely managed to escape the tail end of the scandals that had put an end to his father-in-law's career, if not to his ambitions.

As it turned out, Rocky had been back in the States after a stint in Kosovo when Sullivan had gone down in flames. Still immersed in his own private, personal immolation, he had not joined the pack, choosing instead to watch the coverage from the privacy of his barren apartment. Looking calm, pale and emotionless, Sarah Mariah had been there each day beside her husband and his lawyers. Comparing the grown-up woman to the teenage girl he remembered, he couldn't help but wonder how much it was costing her. God knows, she must have already suffered enough when her father's sins had come home to roost.

Under the most trying circumstances imaginable for any sensitive young woman, she had never, to his knowledge, lost her dignity. Rocky watched as day after day she'd be caught outside and surrounded before she could escape. Head held high, she would face down her tormentors with that same disconcertingly direct gaze he remembered.

"Miz Sullivan, did you know at the time…?"

"No comment."

"Mrs. Sullivan, is it true that you've already filed for divorce?"

"No comment."

"Hey, Sarah, is it true that you were at some of those Georgetown parties your husband threw? Is it true that a Hollywood director supplied the talent and the—''

"If you'll excuse me?"

Someone—Rocky learned later it was her father's

housekeeper—usually rescued her by pulling her bodily away when she would have stood there with that startled-doe look in her eyes until she ran out of no-comments.

After a while the two scandals had run together in his mind: the senator's illegal fund-raising, aka influence peddling, arranging for the bypassing of certain sanctions to sell classified materials to terrorist nations, and the offshore bank accounts; followed only a few years later by Sullivan's sordid little sex, drugs and booze peccadilloes. The consensus was that the man was incredibly stupid to have continued his activities right on through his father-in-law's investigation.

But then Rocky had been immersed in his own private hell while it was all going on. About the time the first scandal was making the nightly news, Julie's kidneys had begun to fail. Dialysis had held her for a while, but under the circumstances, she had not been a candidate for transplant. After one last quick overseas assignment, he had handed in his resignation, needing to spend as much time as he could with the woman he'd once loved.

So it was all mixed up in his mind—the end of his shell of a marriage, the Jones-Sullivan affair, and the end of his career. A man could run only so far, so long, before life caught up with him.

He did recall wondering more than once how the shy, intelligent girl with the wry sense of humor, the haunting little half smile and the marked lack of physical coordination, could have married a lightweight like Sullivan in the first place. The guy was smooth. He had the kind of face the cameras loved, but Rocky had once heard him on a radio talk show when a caller had asked if he was worried about the Chi-coms controlling both ends of the Panama Canal.

Judging by his response, the poor jerk had never heard of the Panama Canal, much less any possible political ramifications. He had stumbled around in search of a response and ended up parroting the day's talking points about campaign finance reform. By the end of the program he'd been batting 0 for 4.

Still, the guy must have had something on the ball. Sarah Mariah had married him. And just as she had stood by her father during the Senate hearings, she had stood stoically beside her husband as, one after another, all his tawdry little secrets had been exposed. With a face that revealed none of her emotions, she had quietly shamed all but the hardcore paparazzi before it was over into granting her grudging respect.

But by that time Rocky had stopped watching. Enough was enough.

Enough was too damned much.

The congressman's sleazy affairs had been too commonplace to sustain a media barrage for long, once it was determined that national security was not at stake. The mess had sprung up again briefly a few months later when Sullivan had taken dead aim at a bridge abutment and totaled both himself and his car. Shortly after that, Sarah Mariah dropped out of sight.

That must have been about the same time that Rocky himself had dropped out. One way of putting it. He had watched Julie's final decline. He had cried. He had read until he couldn't face another book. He'd watched an entire season of baseball, his own brand of opiate. When he'd realized he was drinking too much, he had quit cold turkey. All things considered, it hadn't exactly been a banner year.

A few nights after Dan Sturdivant's retirement party, Rocky was watching the news and toying with the idea of doing a series of columns when he caught a thirty-second teaser for a daytime talk show featuring Binky Cudahy, author of the upcoming bestseller, *The Senator's Daughter's Husband's Other Women.*

That's when it hit him. Wherever she'd gone, whatever kind of a life she had managed to salvage for herself, the congressman's widow was probably going to come in for some unwelcome attention once the book hit the stands. Did she even know about it? Did she watch daytime TV?

For all he knew she might be lying on the sand soaking up sun on some tropical island by now. God knows, she deserved a break.

But she also deserved to know what was headed her way, in case she needed to duck. Rocky knew he could find her. He'd put in too many years as a reporter not to have sources. Although why he should feel this proprietary interest in a woman he'd met only one time, and that more than twenty years ago, he couldn't have said. Maybe because there was a big, gaping hole where his life used to be.

Well, hell…the least he could do was give her fair warning that the buzzards would soon be circling again.

Two

Sarah Mariah flexed her sore hands and examined the newest crop of injuries. The mashed thumb had been yesterday. The sprained little finger several days before that. Today's scratches were only a minor irritation, but honestly, she was going to have to do better. Good thing she'd had her tetanus booster.

All she'd been trying to do was untangle the wild grapevines from the shrubs that had been allowed to grow unchecked for decades. It wasn't as if she'd been tackling a jungle with her bare hands. The shrubs were threatening to lift the eaves, but she couldn't even prune the blamed things until she could get rid of the blasted vines.

Still, if stiff hands and a few scratches were the worst she had to show for today's work, she'd consider herself lucky. She was still scratching chiggers, and last week she'd had to go after a tick in an inaccessible place with a mirror and a pair of tweezers. Living alone had its drawbacks, but the upside definitely outweighed the downside.

She poured herself a glass of milk and made a salsa and mozzarella sandwich on whole grain bread, feeling righteous because she would rather have had a bacon-cheeseburger with fries. Taking her tray into the parlor, she kicked off her shoes and sprawled out in a recliner that was half a century newer than the rest of her great-aunt's furniture. It was one of the few really comfortable pieces in the house.

There was a TV on a spool-legged table. It had died a natural death several years ago and had never been replaced. Sarah had no intention of having it repaired, although she might decide to free up the table for a potted plant. She had a weather radio and a subscription to the *Daily Advance*. Those, plus weekly trips to the grocery store and sporadic trips to the post office filled her needs for contact with the outside world. If World War III or a tornado threatened, she trusted one of the neighbors to warn her.

It had come as no great surprise that her late great-aunt's lifestyle suited her far better than life in suburban D.C. Sarah had hated Washington, hated the whole political scene. But then, she hadn't chosen it, she'd been born into it. And then she'd had the poor judgment to marry into the same circles. She would like to think she had played her role competently, if with a distinct lack of enthusiasm, right to the end.

During her father's ordeal, Stan had been worse than useless. He'd practically fallen apart. On the few nights when he stayed in, he was drunk by the time she served dinner. She hadn't understood at the time why he'd seemed almost panicked. He couldn't possibly have been involved, she'd reasoned, because if he'd been a part of anything illegal they would have quickly discovered it. He'd had flawless manners and the face of a sexy choirboy. That guileless grin alone had brought in the women's votes. He'd seemed so open, so honest—such a refreshing change from all the others. She remembered once trying to reassure him by telling him not to feel guilty, that none of her father's crimes was his fault. His only sin was being married to the senator's daughter.

She'd said it with a smile—or as much of a smile as she could manage—but he hadn't said a word, either in his own defense or hers. Not that she'd expected him to defend her father. What the senator had done was indefensible. But he might at least have absolved her of the guilt of being J. Abernathy's daughter.

He hadn't. A year or so after the Senate hearings, when her husband had started behaving oddly, she had tried to be understanding. After all, it had been an ordeal for him, too. She remembered thinking that once his term ended she would try to talk Stan into selling the house they'd just purchased and not running for office again. They could go somewhere—anywhere—and start over.

Then the dam had burst and it had happened all over again. The same nightmare, only this time it was even uglier. For the first few days she had been in denial. When she'd been forced to confront the truth—when her husband, in a rare sober moment, had confessed to everything—she'd been devastated. Addie, the old housekeeper who was the nearest thing to a mother she'd had since Mariah Jones had died, had been ready to retire to South Carolina with her granddaughter when the senator's troubles had begun. She had stayed on for Sarah's sake and then returned when Stan's scandal had broken, knowing how desperately Sarah would need her.

While every dirty little secret in her husband's life—every secret but one, thank God—had been exposed, the senator had chosen to hole up in a beach house in North Carolina belonging to his friend, lawyer-lobbyist Clive Meadows. There'd been no reason to expect him to stand by her—he'd never been there for her at any other time in her life, but she could have done with a bit of moral support.

Looking back, Sarah knew he'd made the right choice. His presence would only have stirred up the past. One scandal at a time was all she could deal with.

Thank God for Great-Aunt Emma's legacy. Sarah had visited her maternal grandmother's sister several times as a small child and fallen in love with the stark old farmhouse. The tiny community of Snowden, North Carolina was only a short distance off the highway they always took driving down from Washington to Duck, on the Outer Banks, where her father had the use of Clive's palatial beach house.

When her mother had still been living and the two of them used to go to the beach without the senator, they had usually stopped to visit her mother's only relative. On rare occasions they stayed overnight. Sarah had been eleven the last time they'd spent an entire weekend. She remembered waking in the night with a terrible ache in the pit of her belly and being certain she was about to die. Hearing her crying, both Aunt Emma and her mother had hurried to her room.

"Mariah Gilbert, didn't you even tell the child what to expect?" Emma had demanded. Her great-aunt had never liked the senator, and preferred to ignore the fact that her niece had married him.

"They teach that sort of thing at school, Aunt Emma. I'm sure she knows all about it, don't you, darling?"

All Sarah had known was that she was dying. It had been Emma who had explained that her body was preparing her to be a mother. And that, she remembered, had terrified her even more than the bellyache.

But between the two women they had made her understand that what she was feeling, while unpleasant, was perfectly normal. Then Aunt Emma had brought her a cup of hot, sugared and watered-down whisky, while her mother had located and filled an old rubber hot-water bottle.

After that they hadn't stopped as often. Her mother was diagnosed with leukemia, and Sarah had all but forgotten her great-aunt over the next few years. When Mariah had died, Emma had gone to the funeral, driven there and back in a single day by a neighbor. Sarah had had only a few minutes alone with her. J. Abernathy, distraught over the loss of the wife he had neglected for years, had insisted on having his daughter constantly at his side.

The two women had corresponded, though. Sarah had kept every one of her great-aunt's letters. When Emma had died at the age of eighty-four, she'd left her entire estate, consisting of a house, a Hudson automobile up on blocks in the shed, and sixty acres of land, partly wooded, partly under cultivation, to her great-niece, Sarah Mariah.

It was almost as if she'd known that one day soon Sarah would need a place of her own. The senator—he was still called that, even after being forced to retire in disgrace—had the place on Wye River, but he'd given up the Watergate apartment where she'd practically grown up. Sarah and Stan had bought a tiny house in Arlington, but they'd had to sell it to pay his lawyers. To Stan's credit, he wouldn't allow her to go into the small trust she'd received from her mother, much less sell Aunt Emma's house.

Her father had been no help at all, either financially or emotionally, but she hadn't expected anything from that source. In the end, Sarah had been left with the one thing she valued more than anything in the world.

Privacy. A place of her own where she could retreat, where the world couldn't follow. And if that included loneliness, so be it. She had cut off her friends early on during the first scandal—those that hadn't already cut her. Here the neighbors were few, the closest being almost a mile away. If any of them had connected Emma Gilbert's great-niece-who-married-that-nice-congressman with the recent Washington scandals, they never mentioned it. But then, they weren't inclined to drop by for coffee and gossip.

She missed her old friends, missed the volunteer work she'd been doing for years—the children she'd worked with. Now she kept to herself, paid her utility bills and made the monthly payment to the grandparents of her late husband's secret illegitimate daughter.

What Stan had been involved in had been depraved by anyone's standards to the extent that his political future had been shattered beyond repair. One of the participants had been a juvenile at the time. Her name had not been released, but shortly before Stan's fatal wreck she had called to tell him she'd just had his baby and now she needed money. Utterly distraught, Stan had promised to send what he could, even though at the time they'd been scraping the bottom of the barrel to pay for his defense. He had hung up the phone, blurted out the whole pathetic story, then buried his head in Sarah's lap and cried.

"She...she named her K-Kitty. Oh, God, Sarah, what have I done?"

"Shh, we'll deal with it. Maybe when this is all over we can adopt her."

But before they could make any arrangements, Stan had been killed. By then, a sixteen-year-old girl from Virginia Beach who claimed Stan had fathered her child had been the last thing on Sarah's mind.

Somehow she had managed to get through the following days and do all that needed doing. Her father's old friend, Clive Meadows, had been a big help. The day after the funeral, when a man named Sam Pough had called, claiming his daughter had run off and left him and his wife stuck with her bastard, it had actually taken her several minutes to sort it all out.

If Clive had been there at the time, she probably would have simply handed him the phone and let him handle it. Later on, when she'd had time to think, she was glad she'd been alone. She remembered taking so many deep breaths she had grown dizzy. Once her head had cleared, she'd heard herself calmly promising to send an initial sum and make monthly payments as long as the grandparents promised to look after the baby. They were decent, God-fearing people, the man had repeated several times, but their trailer was too old, too small, and their social security would stretch only so far.

Sarah had done the best she could. By liquidating her trust fund, she'd been able to send a sizable check to cover the cost of a new mobile home. Since then she'd sent monthly payments with the understanding that those payments would continue only so long as the child was well cared for and her identity remained a secret. No child, she told herself, should have to grow up bearing the stigma of a father's disgrace.

As time passed with no further contact from the Poughs, Sarah had made herself learn to relax. It wasn't that easy, in spite of having left the past behind and moved to the country. Growing up as her father's daughter, she'd been expected to dress a certain way, to behave a certain way—to go to the right schools, the right summer camps—to smile at appropriate moments, and to express herself only on noncontroversial topics.

Once she'd become the congressman's wife there had been a whole new set of expectations. Never once had anyone asked her personal opinion on an important issue. And she most definitely did have opinions, on any number of issues. Nor did they agree very often with those of her father or her husband.

Never once in her entire life could she recall being asked how she would have preferred to spend her vacations. Given a choice, she might have chosen to attend a fiddlers' convention with her college friends, sleeping in tents, wandering from campfire to campfire listening to the music, sharing food and easy companionship. Instead, she had spent every vacation with one or both of her parents, usually at Clive's beach house, surrounded by other adults.

Instead of flying lessons, she had taken piano lessons. Instead of choosing her own friends, she'd had appropriate ones chosen for her, at least until she'd gone off to school.

It wasn't that her childhood had been unhappy, it was just that she'd never been allowed off the leash long enough to discover who she was. And now that she was free to be herself, she didn't know where to begin, other than wearing thrift-shop jeans, going barefoot and drinking water from her own tap instead of what her Aunt Em had called store-bought water. After a lifetime of pleasing others, she had only herself to please, and the most rebellious thing she had done so far was to stay up half the night reading and then sleep until noon the next day.

These days she couldn't even manage that. Since she'd started on the long-overdue yard work, tackling one square foot at a time, she was usually so tired she fell asleep in the recliner.

Dull was a matter of degrees. Her life had always been—well, until a little over two years ago—dull, as in *boring*. Now it was dull as in *restful*. As in taking time to sniff the roses, not to mention the honeysuckle and corn tassels and whatever else grew in the country. As in trying her hand at writing and illustrating a special story for a little girl she would probably never even get to see.

But right now—at least once she'd caught her breath—it was time for another attack on that blasted board on her front porch that she'd tripped on at least a dozen times. Tomorrow would be time enough to free the rest of her shrubbery from the strangling clutches of those voracious vines.

After rubbing aloe lotion onto her hands, she picked up the daily paper published in the nearby riverside town. Sipping her milk, she skimmed articles about people she didn't know, who didn't know her. There wasn't a speck of world news, rarely even a political commentary. She liked it that way. She read the obituaries of people she'd never heard of, wedding announcements for young hopefuls who had no idea of the pitfalls ahead. She read notices of fiftieth wedding anniversaries, wondering if the couples knew how fortunate they were, and tried not to feel sorry for herself. Given a choice, she knew she would never go back to her old life.

She read about club meetings and historical reenactments and the progress being made on the town's museum. She read about an art show and a moth-boat regatta and considered attending. Mingling with real people again.

One of these days she was going to have to return to the real world and find work. Find some way to make her liberal arts degree support her, because Kitty's needs would continue to grow—clothes and schools and health insurance. Her trust fund wouldn't last much longer at the rate she was depleting it, but she refused to accept a penny from her father. Not that he'd offered. Where J. Abernathy Jones was concerned, every penny came with strings attached.

One string, she suspected, led to Clive Meadows. She'd known Clive for years. It was his beach house they always used. She had met only one of his three wives and been shocked that the girl was so young.

Not surprisingly, she rarely liked her father's friends. Clive was no better, no worse than most. Once, before she'd married Stan, when Clive was between wives, he had asked her out to dinner. She had declined. A few nights later he'd invited her to a concert. She had thanked him and pleaded another engagement.

Her father had been in Scotland when Stan had been killed in a one-man accident that had been deemed a suicide. Clive had been there to offer comfort and professional advice, to steer her through the formalities. At the time she had gratefully accepted his help.

But as for anything more, Sarah, at age thirty-seven, was far too old for a man of his tastes—his wives had been barely out of their teens. Of course, she might have imagined his interest. Distraught, she could easily have read too much into a few innocent shoulder pats, a few avuncular hugs and the offer, after Stan's private memorial service, of a quiet month at his beach house at Duck.

At any rate, she was safe now, and as long as she could continue paying for Kitty's needs and stretch what was left to cover the necessities—food, books, utilities and property taxes—she intended to stay put. Loneliness was a small price to pay for peace of mind.

Rocky rounded a sharp curve on the narrow highway, humming along with something or other by Sibelius. Years out of practice, he hit only about every fifth note correctly, but then, that was between him and the composer, and the old guy wasn't complaining.

He felt good about what he was doing. Righteous, in fact, which was a big improvement over feeling nothing. Thank God something had come along to drag him out of his lair.

It had already occurred to him that someone else might have already warned her. But in case they hadn't, she needed to know what was about to hit the fan. It probably wouldn't amount to much more than a few jokes on Leno and Letterman, a few sound bytes and film clips—maybe a rehash in the tabloids. After a week at most, the whole thing would die a natural death, but meanwhile, a heads-up might be appreciated.

Besides which, he'd needed a mission. Lately he'd been aware of a growing sense of restlessness. The trouble with being a retired journalist was that the brain refused to retire.

Okay, so he would warn the widow and while he was in the area he might look around for something to quicken his interest. Frontline reporting from the agricultural scene? He could do an investigative piece on the pork industry, maybe hang it on the hook of environmental pollution versus genetic engineering. Would reshuffling a few pig genes render hog lagoons obsolete?

He whistled along with the familiar theme of "Finlandia" and wondered how long it had been since he'd whistled. Or hummed anything. Once an enthusiastic sing-alonger, it had been years since he'd been enthusiastic about anything.

When his watch beeped at noon, he switched off the CD and turned on the news.

"—at Camp David. The meeting is scheduled to cover—" He changed stations and caught the tail end of a report on the latest airline disaster, waited through a string of commercials and heard the farm report. Nothing about the Cudahy book. Maybe he'd overestimated the threat. It might not show up at all in this particular market. Even so, it was about time for the publisher to start chumming the waters if they hoped to see people lined up outside the bookstores, money in hand, on laydown day.

Meanwhile, he'd do well to work on his tactics. "Mrs. Sullivan, I'm an independent journalist, and I've come to warn you about—"

Yeah, right. Considering what she'd been put through these past few years, that might not be the best approach. Direct was his favored method, but direct in this case would probably get him kicked out on his keester. The lady had no reason to welcome the press.

Of course, it wasn't too late to call it off. He could go back to Chevy Chase, refreshed from spending a day in the country, and either watch a few more ball games or start on his version of the Great American novel. The story of how one cynical journalist, semi-retired, discovered a way to put an end to all turf wars, ethnic vendettas and ideological battles.

But as long as he was in the neighborhood, he might as well pay his respects to Mrs. Sullivan. Maybe she'd offer him a cup of tea.

Or a cream cheese sandwich.

Finding her had been easy enough. He was not, after

all, without investigative skills. According to the ex-senator's yard man, she had not been to the Wye River place in nearly a year. None of her former friends had offered a clue—of course, they might have been in protective mode. Taking the next logical step, he had checked out public records. Wills, taxes, tax maps.

Bingo. If he could do it, it was a sure bet he wouldn't be the only one. Sleazy exposés were a dime a dozen. They seldom changed the course of history, but they could generate a few column inches in the tabloids and make life miserable for the victims before they were bumped off the lists by the next contender.

Discounting their one brief encounter, Rocky really didn't know Sarah Mariah Jones Sullivan at all. By now she might even welcome the attention. But if she was anywhere as vulnerable as she'd looked during the hearings—as she'd struck him that day over twenty years ago when she'd watched her father use her and discard her as casually as he would a soiled tissue— then maybe she could use a friend.

And if he happened to have guessed wrong about which way she'd jumped—if she was kicking up her heels in some fancy resort instead of hibernating in corn country—no problem. He'd needed an excuse to get out. Needed to start getting involved again.

Slowing down, he took the Snowden turnoff, rounded a blind curve on a narrow blacktop, crossed over a railroad track and began looking for a dirt road that led off to the right. The only sign of life was a big buck deer and a flock of gulls following a tractor, reminding him that they were only a mile or so from Currituck Sound.

He spotted the dirt road and turned off, driving

slowly. Tax maps didn't reveal a whole lot of detail, but there was supposed to be another road of some sort.

And there it was. Two leaning posts, one supporting a newspaper box, the other a mailbox. The name on the mailbox said Gilbert, which, if memory served, was the name of the relative whose house Sarah had inherited. Rocky pulled off the road and parked behind a dusty red compact. After a moment's hesitation he set the brake, locked his eight-year-old SUV and set out on foot down the winding, rutted lane. He'd gone barely a dozen yards when he spotted a guy armed with a videocam jogging toward the house.

Evidently his suspicions had been justified. The lady was about to find herself in the crosshairs again. "Yo! You with the camera!"

The guy glanced over his shoulder, but instead of stopping, he picked up speed. It occurred to Rocky that he could be an innocent nature photographer— maybe a stringer for some hunting-fishing rag. He didn't think so, though. There was something a little too furtive about the way he kept checking his six.

One thing he'd learned during a career that spanned more than two decades was that while photos could easily lie—and people often did, intentionally or not— the subconscious mind was the closest thing to a truth detector any man possessed. *If* he knew how to use it.

The other fellow had the advantage of youth and a head start. Halfway down the lane, Rocky planted his feet and used his fingers to issue a shrill whistle. Occasionally the unexpected trumped any advantage.

At the sound, the photographer came to a dead halt. Roland "Rocky" Waters stood in the middle of a country lane and wondered, Okay, what now, Rambo?

Three

Damn blasted board. It should have been replaced years ago, just as the gutters should have been repaired or replaced. Aunt Emma had been in her eighties, for heaven's sake. Sarah should have come down here and seen to all the repairs, herself. At least she could have hired someone.

But she hadn't. Too wrapped up in her own woes. And now everything needed fixing. Whether she sold the house, which would break her heart, and moved back to the city to find work, or turned the place into a bed and breakfast catering to people looking for a place in the slow lane—in this case, the *very* slow lane—things needed doing. She tackled them one after another.

Yesterday it had been the grapevines, which she still hadn't finished. Today it was the board she stubbed her toe on every time she walked down to this end of the porch. Clutching the hammer just behind the head, she glanced up at the sound of a car out on the road. It was so quiet she could hear for miles...not that there was much to hear. Crows. Farm equipment. Now and then a barking dog.

Between cornfields that had been leased out to the same farmer for years, the overgrown shrubbery and the tall, longleaf pines that shed all over the roof, clogging the gutters, she couldn't see as far as the dirt road, much less the blacktop. Later on, during hunting season, she might see half a dozen hunters, even though her land was posted.

The man jogging toward her house didn't look like a hunter. Nor did he look lost. In fact, she thought uneasily as she sat back on her heels, scowling against the sun's glare, with that big camera thing he was carrying, he looked suspiciously like one of the flock of vultures that had once made her life such a living hell.

What on earth could have happened to bring the press down on her head *this* time? Surely the Poughs hadn't gone public, not after all this time. That would be killing the golden goose. She hadn't missed a single payment, and while it wasn't much, it was the best she could do.

It occurred to her that it had been weeks since she'd spoken to her father. If something had happened to him, surely someone would have called her. She didn't like the man, certainly didn't trust him and wouldn't particularly care if she didn't have to see him for the next few years, but she supposed she still loved him. Daughters were supposed to love their fathers, and if nothing else, she'd been trained to be a dutiful daughter.

By now she had a pretty clear view of her visitor. He was no one she'd ever seen before, of that she was certain. He certainly didn't look like anyone her father would have sent after her.

Still on her hands and knees, Sarah tried to make up her mind what to do. She had learned the hard way to avoid confrontation whenever possible, but to stand her ground when escape was not an option. She was still trying to make up her mind when a shrill whistle split the air.

A *whistle?* What in God's name was going on?

And then a second man came into sight around the curve in her rutted, overgrown lane. Clutching the hammer, she almost forgot to breathe. Something must have happened—something awful. Maybe someone was in trouble. Maybe there'd been an accident out on the highway. Maybe someone needed her help—or at least, her telephone.

"Miz Sullivan?" The first man was panting, clearly out of shape. At closer range, he appeared younger than the man following him. The second man, taller, darker, slightly older, sprinted forward, grabbed his arm and swung him around.

Sarah scrambled to her feet. "Just what is going on?" she demanded at the same time the older man began to speak.

"Didn't you see the signs? This is private property," she heard him say. Well built, he was wearing jeans and a khaki shirt—standard wear for the locals. Did she know him? Was he a neighbor she hadn't yet met?

"Both of you, stop right there!" She lifted the hammer as a warning. "My land is posted and you're trespassing."

"You heard what the lady said." The dark-haired stranger was still holding on to the younger man's camera arm. At closer range, he didn't look particularly dangerous. All the same, she'd learned to be wary.

Oddly enough, it was his eyes she noticed most as the two men came closer. They reminded her of the icy fjords she had seen on her one and only trip to Scandinavia.

"Hey, get off my back, man, I was here first! Miz Sullivan, what do you think about the book—"

"The lady has no comment." By that time both men had reached the gate at the foot of her front walk.

The younger man wore a headband and a ponytail. Attempting to elbow his pursuer away, he whined, "Hey, butt out, old man, this is my story."

"There's no story here. The lady says you're trespassing. You want a story? Try the county courthouse. Oldest one in the state. Fascinating history."

By now they were halfway up the walk, almost at her front steps. Sarah Mariah had had enough. "I'm calling the sheriff," she warned, and turned to go inside. That's when her foot caught the board she'd been repairing. She flung out her hands to catch herself, and the hammer flew across the porch and landed at the feet of the man with the ponytail.

"Jeeze, lady, you don't have to get physical, I can take a hint." He backed away, muttering under his breath.

Sarah was hurting too much to care what was being

said. She hadn't actually seen stars, but close enough. Rubbing her forehead where she'd struck the edge of the screen door, she tried to assess the damage. The very last thing she needed when she was in klutz mode was a pair of witnesses.

The younger man was halfway down the lane. He was shaking his head. The older man came up onto the porch. "Are you all right? That was a pretty serious crack you took."

Up close, he was even better looking. She had learned the hard way not to trust men who were too good-looking. This one wore the shadow of a beard, which might or might not be a fashion statement. There was a certain watchful quality about him, as if he weren't quite sure of his welcome.

Smart man. "Who are you? What do you want?"

"You've forgotten already? It's only been, what—twenty years?"

"Have we met?" She tried to ignore the pain, but both her eyes were beginning to water. Even so, if she had ever met this man before, she would have remembered. His was not the kind of face a woman could ever forget.

Although on closer examination, there *was* something about him. Something about his eyes...pale gray, set off by thick black lashes and eyebrows. Where had she seen such eyes before?

He seemed almost to be waiting for her to recognize him, but at the moment her head hurt too much to think. "Twenty years?" she repeated. "I'm sorry, but—"

"More like twenty-two, I guess. Rocky Waters,

Mrs. Sullivan. And you were Miss Anonymous Jones. The king was having a bad hair day, remember?''

Rocky Waters, Rocky Waters, Rocky…

Oh, blast and tarnation. "The tea and cream cheese."

"Managed to salvage my shoes, but you know what? You're going to have a beauty of a shiner. Maybe if you put something on it before the swelling starts?''

"The swelling," she repeated, sounding almost as dazed as she felt. It was partly the crack on her forehead, partly the fault of the man standing before her.

To think of all the hours she'd wasted after that one brief meeting thinking about him. Daydreaming. Creating wild, adolescent fantasies about someone she'd met only once, and then in the most embarrassing circumstances. Seeing him now, years later and out of context, it had taken a few minutes to connect. He looked more than ever like one of those dark, dangerous Black Ops heroes in her favorite romantic suspense novels.

God knows what she must look like after a day of wrestling grapevines—with one eye rapidly swelling shut.

No point in hoping he hadn't noticed. Taking her by the arm, he said, "You took a real whack there. Let's go inside—you'd better sit while I get a towel and some ice. Don't suppose you have an ice bag, do you?''

"An ice bag?''

"Thought not. You don't look like the type.''

"What type?" Pain was beginning to radiate from her eye socket all the way down to her jawbone. Momentarily dazed into compliance, she let him lead her inside. ''Straight through there,'' she said, her voice now little more than a strained whisper. He pulled out a kitchen chair, and she lowered herself carefully, then watched as he removed a tray of ice from the avocado-green refrigerator, a relic of the last time her great-aunt had modernized her kitchen.

''Hangovers. Bet you've never had one in your life, have you?''

''No—actually, yes.'' There were a lot of things she'd never done and now probably never would, but he didn't have to know it. ''Clean towels are in there.'' She pointed at the drawer where she kept kitchen linens. ''Why are you doing this? Why are you even here?''

Rocky took the time to crack the ice with a meat tenderizer he found in a drawer along with three emergency candles, a ball of string and a few dozen rubber jar rings.

Why was he here? Good question. He'd set out with honorable intentions—mostly honorable, anyway. Warn the lady of what was in the pipeline. Help her with a preemptive strike, but only if she thought it would help defuse the situation.

As for him, part of the problem was that he'd been unable to motivate himself into getting back to writing after Julie's death. If the senator's daughter needed his help, he would give it his best shot.

If not…no problem. He'd warn her of what to expect because he'd seen too many victims blindsided after a tragedy by having a camera and a mike shoved in their face unexpectedly. Warn her, wish her luck and leave.

At the moment, however, he didn't think she was in any shape to hear what he'd come to say. "Here, hold this against your face."

She took the ice-filled towel and placed it gingerly against her eye. "You were a lot younger then," she said. "I seem to remember that our whole conversation was like something out of *Alice in Wonderland.*"

"Right. We were both younger. So…how's Toto?"

"Still in Kansas. Wrong story."

He grinned, managing to look both raffish and kind. "Just wanted to be sure you didn't have a concussion. Want to count my fingers?" He waggled them in front of her face.

"Not really. Are you here for any particular reason? Nobody just drops in because they happen to be in the neighborhood. There isn't any neighborhood, in case you failed to notice."

Sarah wondered if she'd broken the skin. Along with the throbbing, her eyebrow was starting to sting. "You're hovering," she grumbled. "I hate it when someone hovers. If you have something to say, then say it and leave. Please."

"I came to warn you about the book."

She dropped the towel. It came unfolded, and ice scattered across the linoleum. Ignoring it, she tried to focus on the man with one good eye and one that was rapidly swelling shut.

"The book. Right. Which one are we talking about this time, Oz or Alice? No don't bother—the joke's beginning to wear thin." She wanted him to go so that she could give in to the pain. Curse or cry, or at least wallow in self-pity. All of which were luxuries she could only now afford to indulge.

Instead of leaving, he pulled out a chair and sat, uninvited. Then he proceeded to tell her why he'd gone to the trouble of tracking her down. This time the book wasn't *The Wizard* and it wasn't *Wonderland*. It was...

"The Senator's Daughter's Husband's Other Women? Tell me you're making that up." In stunned disbelief, Sarah heard him out. "She can't do that...can she?"

But of course she could. Having spent practically her entire life in Washington, Sarah well knew how each major scandal was rehashed in books that hit the stands in record time. The only curious thing was that this one had taken so long.

Dear God, what if the Poughs thought she was somehow benefiting from her late husband's notoriety and demanded more money? She was already sending as much as she could afford. Even worse, what if, on seeing the Cudahy woman cash in on a rehash of the whole wretched mess, they decided to go public with Kitty's secret? How much would the tabloids pay for something like that? Pictures of an innocent child under the caption, Disgraced Congressman's Secret Lovechild.

Lifting her battered face, she whispered, "Why is that awful woman doing this? If she was actually there—if she was one of the...the—"

"Sluts," Rocky provided.

"How can she be so brazen?"

He shrugged. "Money. Her fifteen minutes of fame. Who knows?"

Sarah placed the wet towel on the table and rubbed her fingers together. They were cold. She felt cold all over. Felt as if she were trapped inside one of those snowstorm paperweights that someone had just given a good, hard shake.

She studied the man seated across the table. He had changed in some ways—twenty-odd years could do that to anyone. He'd been a brand-new reporter when she'd first met him. Her adolescent crush had eventually faded, but she'd gone on following his career, seeing him occasionally on TV covering some foreign affairs flap, reporting from overseas or doing a segment on one of the Sunday talk shows. Somewhere along the line he seemed to have dropped out of sight, but by that time she had already begun playing ostrich.

She had to wonder now if his intentions were quite as innocent as he wanted her to believe.

Carefully she replaced the towel, now minus most of the ice but still cold and comforting. She'd been a fool, living in her pretty bubble, believing herself insulated from the rest of the world. Just because she had stopped keeping up with the news didn't mean the rest of the world had ceased to exist. It was still out there, like a big, hungry bear waiting to devour the unwary. She'd gone into hibernation, and now the bear had followed her into her cave.

"But why?" she asked again. "Sorry. If it sounds as if I'm whining it's because I am."

"You're entitled. Go ahead, whine if it helps, but maybe you'd better take an aspirin first. That bruise is going to be pretty uncomfortable for a while."

It already hurt like the very devil, but she knew better than to show weakness before the enemy, whoever and whatever the enemy in this case was. If the bear was out there, then this man, for all she knew, could be the bear's emissary. "I'll do that. And thank you—I guess. You've warned me what to expect."

"You might want to take a vacation until things blow over."

"Good idea." It would be a good idea if she could afford it. "Do you mind telling me how you found me?"

Briefly he explained about public records, private sources and the powers of deduction. She sighed, knowing that in these days of instant high-tech intelligence it was almost impossible for anyone to disappear without a trace. "If I'd known this was going to happen I might have tried to get into the witness protection program." Her rueful smile was probably more of a grimace, but it was the best she could do. "Maybe I'll get myself a junkyard dog."

"Unless you're used to handling junkyard dogs, he'd be more of a threat than a benefit."

"Well, what would you do in my place?"

He was leaning against the white-painted counter, looking dark and dangerous against the glass-fronted cabinets. The man was simply too big, too masculine, too...tough wasn't quite the right word, but it would do until a better one occurred. She had a feeling that those deceptively clear eyes of his hid a wealth of secrets. And she didn't want to share his secrets, she really didn't. She had enough of her own.

Once, a long time ago, he had been carelessly kind to a fifteen-year-old girl who'd been bored, discouraged, hurt and sorely in need of a friendly smile.

He wasn't smiling now. And kind or not, she had no real reason to trust him. "Did you come here for an exclusive?"

He appeared to consider his answer. "Would you believe me if I said no?"

Sarah knew to her sorrow that entire careers sometimes hung on a single word spoken at the wrong time, to the wrong ears.

Where was your husband on Labor Day weekend?

Labor Day? He was in Michigan, doing a town hall thing.

He said he was home with you, just the two of you, that you'd dismissed your housekeeper and cooked out and then watched a movie on TV.

She'd never been a good liar. It had never occurred to her that she even needed to lie until it was too late. Far too late. So she said nothing.

Rocky watched a series of subtle expressions pass over the widow's face. He was good at reading faces. She was far better than most when it came to concealing her thoughts, but he'd caught her off guard, in a vulnerable position. "Has it occurred to you that you could get the jump on the Cudahy woman by coming out first with your own version of what happened?"

Four

Rocky shoved away from the counter, the motion bringing him just close enough to her chair that he could smell…insect repellent? Shampoo? Under other circumstances he might have touched her on the shoulder in a wordless gesture of comfort before leaving, but something told him that touching this woman would be a mistake.

While she gingerly fingered the lump on her brow, he studied the changes that had taken place since his one and only up-close and personal look. Considering all she'd gone through since then, she had changed surprisingly little. Same great cheekbones. Same expressive eyes. Same mouth—a bit large, given to quick smiles, as quickly withdrawn. Total package? Hardly spectacular, but…nice.

He remembered the expression in her eyes then—a

certain sadness, a wariness. It had changed very little over the years. Grown warier, if anything. With good cause.

Funny, the way a retentive mind could trap a few insignificant details and file them away for years. A smile—a way of tilting the head that indicated a healthy skepticism. No reason why any of it should have stuck with him all these years, but oddly enough it had.

She fingered her swelling eye gingerly. "I think this is what our old housekeeper would call an ouchie."

"An 'ouchie'? My old man would have called it a shiner." His old man was such a dim and distant memory that he had no idea what he would have called it. It was something to say, that's all. Small talk—something he'd never been particularly good at.

"I've never had a black eye before." Her look was one of pride mingled with dismay. He found it oddly disarming.

She was a mess, all right. No makeup, ragbag clothes—pine straw in her hair, scratches on her hands and a brand-new shiner bursting into full bloom. There was nothing even faintly seductive about the woman, yet he found himself looking at her in a way he hadn't looked at any woman in years.

Which one, he wondered, was the real Sarah Mariah Jones Sullivan? The awkward adolescent who'd been used countless times as a stage prop by her father and then ignored? Or the self-possessed woman who had stood at his side while his empire crumbled, then been forced to do the same thing for her husband a few years later under even more embarrassing circumstances?

Or this fragile creature with the leaves in her hair, perspiration stains on her shirt and a dripping towel covering half her face?

She might look fragile, but there was a surprising degree of strength, not to mention courage, inside that delicate frame. He remembered watching the news coverage both times. She'd always tried to slip away unnoticed, but once the pack had her cornered she would stand her ground and politely answer each question until someone—probably the housekeeper she'd mentioned—managed to rescue her.

The same woman was standing not three feet away, looking no less composed despite baggy jeans, a sweaty, green-stained T-shirt and hair that might have been styled by a wind tunnel. It occurred to him that for a journalist who knew better, he was beginning to take a dangerously personal interest.

"Well, hey, why don't I just leave now? I've warned you what's about to hit the fan. Handle it any way you want to."

"No, wait—please?" She held out her hand. It was red, the thumb badly bruised. There was a beaded line on the back where she'd evidently scratched herself and the blood had dried.

What the devil was she doing here, digging herself a bomb shelter?

In spite of his better judgment, Rocky settled back against the counter and waited. She stood, stepped on a piece of melting ice, recovered her balance and grimaced. "You might not believe this," she said ruefully, "but I've actually been known to walk across a room without either tripping or spilling anything."

"No kidding." Rocky thought he might have underestimated her looks. The lady might not win any beauty contests, but there was something about her that stuck in a man's mind....

Which was why he was here in the first place. "Tell you what," he proposed. "While you take care of damage control, why don't I make us a pot of coffee? If you'll tell me where to find sandwich makings, I can put together something to stave off the wolf, and we'll talk over our options."

Our options? He'd meant to say hers. She didn't jump at the offer, but then, he could hardly blame her for being wary. A journalist who had come to warn her about journalists? Maybe she should skip over Alice and Oz and go directly to *Little Red Riding Hood and the Big Bad Wolf.*

It was getting late. Sarah had had breakfast early. Had she eaten lunch or not? Suddenly—illogically—she was starved. The trouble with her new lifestyle was that there was nothing to mark the days, much less the hours. As often as not, she'd work until she was famished, then gobble down whatever was handiest. Or read half the night away and find herself having breakfast at four in the morning.

"Tomatoes on the windowsill, bread in the breadbox. Look in the refrigerator if you want anything else. If you'll excuse me, I need to go—to go..."

Rocky thought he'd better warn her before she confronted a mirror. "Sarah, don't be discouraged by the way it looks now, because—"

"That bad, hmm?" She laughed, shook her head, grabbed her forehead and winced.

Conquering the second urge in as many minutes to

reach out and touch her, he said, "Because it's going to look a hell of a lot worse before it looks better."

"Then maybe *one* of us had better cover our eyes," she said with that same droll sense of humor he remembered from twenty years earlier. "I like my coffee strong, and I want onions and lots of salt and pepper on my sandwich."

Sarah hurried to the bathroom, closed the door behind her and leaned against it. Had she lost her mind? Why had she even allowed him in the house? She knew who he was—or at least, *what* he was. And, whether or not he'd been one of the pack that had hounded her so mercilessly, by now he had to know every sordid detail about her marriage. And like everyone else, he would have drawn the same conclusion. That she'd been such an abject failure as a woman she hadn't even been able to hold her husband's interest.

By the time she returned to the kitchen, he'd made sandwiches, cut them neatly and placed them on a platter. The table was set with Aunt Emma's moss rose plates, cups and saucers and her old-fashioned silver. Almost everything in the house was just the same as it had been for the past forty-odd years—the same appliances in the same sickly shade of green. The same yellow enameled table and uncomfortable straight chairs painted to match. The same wag-tailed clock that was too big for the wall space and consistently slow.

It all looked the same. Until a few minutes ago it had even felt the same. It was nowhere near as luxurious as the apartment where she'd grown up, or even the far more modest house she had shared with Stan.

But for some reason she'd always felt secure here, even as a child.

Now even that had changed.

They ate first and were on their second cups of coffee before either of them brought up his reason for being there. Sarah took a deep breath and said, "It's probably not that big a deal—the book, I mean. After all, it's been a year since Stan—since he—and even longer since my father resigned." She didn't add "in disgrace." It wasn't necessary. "People will have forgotten by now."

"Don't count on it."

She knew better than to count on anything. Or anyone. "Well, what do you recommend, that I go somewhere off the beaten track and wait it out? Or buy myself a vicious dog? Or maybe I could build an electric fence around the entire yard."

Rocky glanced out the kitchen window at the surrounding cornfields and pine woods. Off the beaten track? Was she kidding? "I mentioned issuing a preemptive strike."

"Meaning?"

"Meaning coming out just ahead of the Grand Teton's book with—"

"*Whose* book?"

"Sorry. The name she goes by is Binky Cudahy, but her nickname is—" he cleared his throat "—well, you get the idea."

"She's well endowed, I take it?" Sarah said dryly.

"Let's just say when the sun's directly overhead, her feet are in the shade." He thought he detected a twitch at the corners of her mouth, but he wasn't about to jeopardize any progress he might have made toward disarming her.

"Suppose you tell me the worst that can happen, and I'll decide whether or not I need to take evasive action."

Point by point, he laid out the facts. The book was compiled from material supplied by one Belinda aka Binky Cudahy. It included explicit firsthand accounts of a number of sordid parties involving the usual array of sex, drugs and booze. The only thing that made it worth the gutter press's attention was that the parties had included several Hollywood names as well as that of a young congressman who had once shown promise of being a rising star.

A star, perhaps, Rocky acknowledged silently, but never a statesman. Since the advent of television, intellect had become less a requisite for getting elected than having a marketable personality and the ability to generate good sound bytes. Sullivan had been glib, plus he possessed the kind of clean-cut good looks that had made him a favorite with women voters. Better yet, he'd had excellent connections. With the right handlers he might have gone far. Might eventually even have overcome the stigma of being J. Abernathy's son-in-law, if he hadn't screwed up. In Rocky's opinion, the jerk had deserved what had happened to him.

His widow didn't.

"How long will it take before it blows over?" she asked thoughtfully. Late-afternoon light cast tantalizing shadows on her elegant throat, triggering an aberrant reaction. Rocky found himself wondering how her skin would feel, smell, taste. Warm and slightly moist? Sweet or slightly salty?

Hauling his brain back in line, he said brusquely, "My guess, you'll have a week before and maybe another week after the book hits the stores. These postmortems never last long unless there's an ongoing investigation."

"Why did you bother to track me down and warn me?"

Toying with the salt shaker, he gave it some thought. When she put it to him that way, he didn't honestly know. Maybe because throughout all the floods and famines, the insurrections, revolutions and shaky peace negotiations he had covered in the years since sharing their single previous meeting, he had never quite forgotten a klutzy, embarrassed kid who had struck him as painfully lonely. She wouldn't want to hear it any more than he cared to admit it, but there it was. Considering the places he'd been, the things he had witnessed in the intervening years—including saying a final goodbye to his wife—it didn't make sense that he still remembered that one brief episode. That one vulnerable adolescent girl.

Raking back his chair, he rose and took his plate and cup to the sink. "Anything I can do before I leave?"

She appeared to consider it. "I don't suppose you'd care for a job as a handyman? No, don't answer, I couldn't afford you, anyway."

"You don't know my rates yet."

"Actually, I enjoy staying busy. I'll just go on tackling things one at a time and eventually everything will get done."

"By then it'll all need doing again." Rocky was aware of another conversation going on at another level. He wondered if she felt it, too.

I'm uneasy. I'm not quite sure why, but I wouldn't mind if you hung around a little longer.

Maybe I should. Maybe you need me but you're too proud to admit it.

Crazy. After six months of self-imposed solitude, now he was hearing voices inside his head. "Guess I'd better hit the road while there's still some daylight left," he said abruptly.

As they stood there sharing the awkward moment, it occurred to Rocky that she was taller than he remembered. She'd been skinny then, but not quite so fragile. Obviously the past few years had taken a heavy toll.

"Well...thank you again for warning me. And for running that reporter away. I truly doubt if any more will show up. Stan's gone, my father's not here and I've never done anything more newsworthy than smear cream cheese and asparagus on the shoes of a world-famous journalist."

"World-famous, huh? Move over Bret, Tony and Sam."

She followed him outside and he leaned down to pick up the hammer she'd dropped and placed it in her hand. "Show me how you use this thing."

"What?" She goggled at him.

Grinning, he turned back to the porch, to the swollen board she'd been trying to force back in place and nail. "Go ahead, hit the nail."

Looking at him as if he might have lost his mind—which was a distinct possibility—she adjusted her grip on the hammer and tapped the nail. It tilted, but didn't go in any deeper.

"Didn't you ever study physics?"

"No, I studied history, literature, art and music. Maybe I should have taken a class in carpentry."

He took the hammer from her hand, holding it an inch from the end of the handle instead of an inch from the business end, as she had. "I'm talking about leverage."

"Leverage I know about," she said, again with the funny little half smile he remembered so well. "As in, vote for my bill or I'll let the press know that you once ran over an endangered species and never bothered to report it."

He laughed and then he took her hand and placed it where his had been on the handle. At the feel of his hard, dry hand on hers, Sarah caught her breath and held it. "Hold it like this," he instructed. "No, don't choke up on it. Now go ahead, swing it and hit the nail. You'll never get the job done if you don't know how to use tools properly."

She tried it. Missed the nail, but hit the board with a resounding, satisfying whack. The smile she gave him hurt her face, but there was no holding back. "Oh, I see what you mean about leverage. Well…thank you again for the warning and the carpentry lesson. And the sandwich."

"My pleasure." He hesitated a moment, then touched her on the shoulder, wished her luck and was halfway down the front walk when a car turned off the state road into the lane.

No need to ask if it was someone she knew. Rocky could tell by the stricken look on her face that whoever it was, her visitor was about as welcome as another black eye. He waited a moment, studying the car and driver. Ten to one, it was another representative of the gutter press. If one of the buzzards had tracked her down, the rest of the flock wouldn't be far behind.

Swearing, he turned in his tracks and jogged back to where Sarah still stood on the porch. "Get inside, I'll handle it."

Without a word of protest, she went inside and watched through the screen door as a second car turned into the lane, slowed down and stopped behind the first. My God, she thought, that makes three. It never occurred to her to include Rocky.

Standing on the front steps, arms crossed over his chest, he was truly an impressive figure. Tall, muscular, but not grotesquely so—those measuring eyes and the juggernaut jaw alone would have stopped most people in their tracks.

With everything at stake—Kitty's future peace of mind, her own cozy cocoon, Sarah was amazed to find herself thinking more about the man himself than about the impending threat. Which said a lot about the effects of eleven months of self-imposed solitude, leavened with a few leftover adolescent fantasies.

To think she had begun to feel safe. She had taken such comfort in knowing that the ugliness couldn't reach her here. What possible connection could there be between a widow living alone in northeastern North Carolina, a baby in Virginia Beach and a couple of stale political scandals in Washington, D.C.?

It wasn't going to happen, not if she had to take on the entire fourth estate. She could handle whatever they wanted to dish out, as long as they kept Kitty out of it.

Halfway down the lane, the men talked—Rocky and a scraggly character she would have recognized anywhere as a reporter. Not the type from one of the major outlets, who knew to within an inch how far they could go without getting into trouble with the law. This was the muckraking type that peered into bedroom windows, pawed through garbage cans—the kind that might even use illegal means to get a hook on which to hang a story.

"Just stand back, you jerk," she muttered, shading her eyes against the lowering sun. "I've got a hammer and I know how to use it."

A beige van blocked the lane at the turnoff. Both front doors opened and two men stepped out and paused, apparently waiting to see how the creep with a scraggly beard and digital camera fared.

Evidently, whatever Rocky told him convinced him there was no story here, because he shrugged, climbed back into his car and began backing out the lane. Twice he nearly backed into the drainage ditch that bordered the cornfield, but eventually he made it to the end. The pair from the van got out and walked to meet him. The three men conferred briefly, then both vehicles backed out onto the dirt road and left in a cloud of dust.

Sarah stepped back outside. Rocky continued to watch from the middle of the lane until the dust settled, then turned back toward the house. Now, she supposed he would leave, too. He'd done his good deed—done several of them, in fact. Warned her, fed her, doctored her eye and showed her how to get better mileage from Aunt Emma's hammer. Not to mention driving off the bad guys.

"Who were they?" she asked as he rejoined her on the porch. As if she couldn't guess.

"Gutter press."

"I thought as much. They must be hard up for news if they thought anyone would be interested in me. Dullest woman in captivity."

"Captivity? Interesting choice of words." A quick smile warmed his ice-gray eyes to a remarkable degree. "Look at it from their point of view. It's not an election year, OPEC's behaving, there hasn't been a sinking, a crash, a protest or a strike lately. There's no hurricane on the charts, not so much as a tropical depression yet, no terrorist threats, no—well, you get the picture." He'd been about to say, no scandals.

"All the same, there must be something going on. Congress is back in session. Surely someone's larding a few bills."

As if he had every right, Rocky took her arm and steered her back inside. "You think these guys care about real news? Serious stories about real issues aren't what catch shoppers' attention when they're standing in line at the supermarket. Now, you take an asteroid with a message from Zeus, or a cross between a chicken and a three-headed snake—or a close-up of the senator's daughter, who happens to be a congressman's widow—who also happens to be sporting a three-ring shiner, and you've got an instant hit on your hands."

Sarah started to touch her swollen eye and thought better of it. "Oh, Lord, I hadn't thought about that."

What if Rocky hadn't been here? What if she'd

gone to the door and flashbulbs had started popping before she could get away?

How'd you get the shiner, Miz Sullivan?

Who's the new guy in your life, Sarah? Is it true you and your husband shared—

"I think we'd better heat up the coffee and have ourselves a conference."

Five

The conference never got off the launching pad. Sarah asked politely about his work. Rocky answered that he was on sabbatical. It sounded better than telling her he'd quit cold when Julie had died and hadn't been able to find the motivation to go back to work.

He asked if she had any plans to move back to Virginia or her father's retirement home on the Wye River. She told him that as soon as she caught up with her repairs and yard work, she intended to visit every place on the map within a day's drive with a name that intrigued her, starting with Waterlily, Swan Quarter, Spot and Mamie, and then branch out to those with names she couldn't pronounce.

Stalemate. Privacy was obviously a big issue with Sarah Mariah Jones Sullivan. Odd, Rocky mused, the way different people reacted to the presence of any representative of the media. It had been his experience that with some, the less they actually knew, the more they felt compelled to talk. With Sarah it was just the opposite. He'd thought he knew her—at least knew more about her than was generally known, far more than she would like for anyone to know. But the more he watched the subtle changes of expression in those calm hazel eyes, the more he realized that he didn't know her at all.

Still waters?

Maybe. What was that old line from a hit song a few decades back? "Deep down, she was shallow."

He'd be willing to bet that deep down, Sarah Mariah was even deeper. What, he wondered, lay under those still waters? Why would an attractive, sophisticated woman be content to live alone in a backwater community? Who—or what—was she hiding from? Or waiting for?

He could ask, but Sarah Mariah Jones Sullivan was not the kind of woman to open up to a stranger. And Roland "Rocky" Waters wasn't the kind of man to walk away from a mystery.

Stalemate number two.

Quickly Rocky scanned his mental file on the Jones family. If she'd been an abused child, some hint of it would have come out during the investigation. It was public knowledge that her father was a self-centered, unscrupulous scoundrel, but that didn't necessarily make him a rotten family man.

It was also a well-known fact, however, that he'd dragged his daughter with him to all kinds of public appearances, played the role of doting papa for the media, then shoved her aside to fend for herself. Usually—but not always—there was an aide whose job it was to look after her. A widower for some quarter of a century now, the senator golfed, played poker and drank, all in moderation and with unexceptional companions, so far as anyone knew. One of his closest friends was Clive Meadows, a lawyer-turned-lobbyist who happened to have a taste for obscenely young wives. At no time, however, had his name been linked to the senator's daughter. Going over the files, Rocky would have caught something like that.

Just the thought gave him an unpleasant feeling. Actually, the thought of Sarah and any man was surprisingly unsettling, possibly because she'd had such a raw deal her first time out of the gate.

And, yeah, he knew it was her first time. He had done his research well. No journalist went into a situation cold if he could help it.

She'd been kept on a leash, allowed to date in moderation during her senior year at a private girls' school. But even in college her male friends had been vetted by the senator or one of his close personal aides. Usually after half a dozen or so outings with any one guy, the boyfriend dropped out and another contender took his place. The senator, it appeared, hadn't taken any chances with what might turn out to be—and had, in fact been—a prime asset. The intelligent, attractive daughter of an influential politician, a young woman whose impeccable reputation had been closely guarded from the cradle on.

Talk about your feudal systems.

Still, his internal radar was bothering him. Could there be something else here? Something that hadn't been uncovered in any of the various investigations? "Sarah Mariah, tell me about—"

"Heavens, would you look at the time. I can't believe so much has happened since I went out to nail down that blasted board on the front porch."

Rocky interpreted the remark as his cue to leave. Now that he'd done what he'd come to do, there was no real reason to stay any longer. Next time he had an urge to do someone a favor, he wouldn't cut it quite so close. As it was, by the time he'd made up his mind to step in, it had almost been too late.

"I know you're busy. Well...you're probably on your way somewhere..." She looked at the clock, at the toaster and then stared out the window. "But if you'd like to, you could spend the night here, there's plenty of room. I'm not sure where the nearest motel is, but this time of year—tourist season, I mean—you might have trouble finding a room."

The beach season. He'd forgotten they were only a short distance from the Outer Banks. The invitation, coming as it had out of the blue, knocked him off balance for a moment.

He hadn't imagined it, then—that silent, subliminal exchange. "If any more reporters show up, don't answer the door and you won't have to answer any questions."

She nibbled on a ragged nail, then tucked her hand behind her, as if ashamed of getting caught in the act. Rocky felt a few defenses he didn't even know he possessed begin to crumble. "If you're sure you wouldn't mind, then I'd appreciate it," he said, and then had to scramble to rationalize hanging around in a place where watching the corn grow was probably the favorite pastime. "That way I could get an early start tomorrow. I, uh…I thought I'd look around while I'm in the area. Lot of history around these parts, I understand."

Wordlessly she nodded.

"Meanwhile, I can place a call or two and find out what's going on with the book so you'll have a heads-up. I doubt if you'll have any more trouble, though."

Rocky could only guess at whether or not he'd reassured her. The more she resorted to that polite little company smile—not the quick half smile he liked so much—the more certain he was that there was something going on here he didn't know about.

Not that it was any of his business. Not that he even had any particular interest, but when a guy went out of his way to do a good deed, the least he could do was hang around long enough to make sure it stuck.

Sarah stood, covered a yawn and murmured an apology. "I'll make up the front room for you. There are fresh towels on the back of the bathroom door. If you need anything else…"

How about some answers?

"No, that sounds great. I'll pull my car in off the road and bring in my bag, if you don't mind."

She made omelets for supper and dusted off a bottle of her great-aunt's homemade wine. Over the simple meal they talked about her situation—at least he did some genteel probing. The lady had learned a lot from her father about the art of obfuscation.

"Are you planning on living here permanently?" he asked after they cleaned up the few dishes and moved into what must once have been called a front parlor.

"I haven't done a lot of long-term planning yet."

"I suppose owning a house helps…financially, I mean."

She nodded and stared out the window at the cornfields that surrounded her house, the tops now gilded by the last gleam of sunset. "Wasn't there a movie a few years back about a baseball diamond in the middle of nowhere, and all these old baseball players coming out of a cornfield?"

"If you're thinking about those reporters, Sarah, it was only four guys. Okay, five, counting me. Don't let it spook you."

"I'm not spooked, I was only…oh, all right. I'll admit that if you hadn't showed up in time to warn me what was happening, I'd have been—well, I wouldn't have panicked, but I might have been—"

"A sitting duck."

"Exactly."

"Delighted to have been of service. Who farms your land?"

"It's been leased to the same farmer for years."

"Provides a pretty good income, huh?"

"Are you prying into my personal finances?"

"Who, me? Would a reporter pry?"

"I thought you said you weren't a reporter any longer."

He shrugged. "I'm not." He held out his hands, palms up. "See? No tape recorder, no notepad—I even left my laptop in the car. I'm not wired, but you could search me if you'd like to." His smile invited her to share the amusement. When she didn't, his own smile faded.

"Could you...write something and send it in if I changed my mind?"

"Do you want me to? There might still be time for a preemptive strike before Cudahy's launch date if we hurry. About all it would do, though, is knock some of the wind out of her sails." The more he thought about it, the more he thought it was a lousy idea.

Seated on a sofa that looked as if it might be padded with concrete, she slipped her hands under her thighs, stared down at the faded floral carpet and rocked from the waist. "No. No, thanks. I'll just ride it out."

"Your choice." He still had contacts. Getting her story out would have been no problem if she'd wanted to go that route. And while it wouldn't have enhanced his own career, or what was left of it—he'd never been that kind of a reporter—he would have done it for her sake, if she'd thought it would help.

There was a story here, all right, only she wasn't ready to open up. He might have lost his edge as a reporter, but that didn't mean all his instincts had shut down.

"I've been thinking of doing some writing, myself," she said after a wheezing old mantel clock struggled through nine asthmatic bongs.

"Is that so?" Oh, hell. She was going to write her own story. Maybe he'd read her wrong.

"I thought maybe a survival guide for aging boomers who want to opt out and live off the land? I mean, now that I know how to use a hammer effectively..." Her smile was the self-deprecating kind, so sweet, so tentative, that he wanted to...touch her. "Pretty silly, isn't it? I majored in English lit, minored in studio art.''

''Oh, I don't know—it sounds like something the back-to-earth types could use. Reading, painting and minor carpentry.''

Rocky told himself that if he had half a grain of sense left, he'd be out of here by now, but what the hell—he could spare one more day.

He could spare a year, but he'd stay another day, maybe two, just until she was over her jitters. Then he'd leave, feeling righteous for having done a good deed for a woman who meant nothing to him personally, with no thought of any personal gain. The tricky part was going to be hanging on to his objectivity. That was only one of the puzzling aspects of this whole crazy affair.

You can handle it, dude. This isn't world politics, just one decent woman who was about to get caught in the flak.

Oh, yeah, he was a real Don Quixote.

Trying not to stare at the darkening bruise on her left eye, he was wondering why such a blemish didn't diminish her essential attractiveness, when the phone rang. Sarah made no move to pick it up.

''Sarah?''

''Let it ring.''

''You know who it is?''

''Probably a salesman.''

Probably not. He had a feeling she knew who was on the other end. He had a feeling she wasn't going to tell him, and that was just fine with him. He was already more involved than he'd planned on being.

After eight rings the phone stopped. A few minutes

later it started up again. This time it fell silent after five rings.

They stared at each other. He knew damned well she was no longer a vulnerable kid. She'd been through enough to have learned how to take care of herself. So why was it he felt this overwhelming compulsion to stay and fight her dragons?

Dragons? A handful of fourth-rate hacks?

Whatever had her so spooked, it was more than a few reporters, more than yesterday's scandals reheated and served up a second time.

Morning in the country was noisy. Crows, seagulls, somebody's rooster and the distant diesel growl of a piece of heavy equipment. Rocky's knowledge of farm life was negligible. He knew the difference between a milking machine and a disc harrow, but that was about as far as it went.

Hearing the sound of the shower, he lay on his back, arms crossed under his head, and absorbed the atmosphere. There was no central air. His room didn't boast a window unit, but with both windows open, it wasn't bad. He'd slept in far worse quarters.

Someone had pinged her window with a BB gun. He wondered if she'd noticed. Wondered if she'd noticed that one of the faded green shutters was barely hanging on by a single rusted hinge. God help her if she was no better on ladders than she was with a hammer. As long as he was here, he might as well check it out.

The shower shut off with a protest of pipes. Unbidden came the vision of a tall, thin woman with hair that could have used a professional cut—with a swollen thumb and a few scratches on the backs of both hands. With small breasts, cheekbones a model would kill for and a mouth that—

Oh, yeah. That mouth was beginning to claim a little too much of his attention. He might have lost some of his objectivity where world politics was concerned, but when it came to women, he was too old, too experienced and far too emotionally insulated to fall for a pair of soft, naked lips.

She was in the kitchen when, freshly shaved, his hair still wet from the shower, he joined her there. For one unguarded moment their eyes met over the yellow enameled table. The quick flair of interest in hers was gone almost before it registered, but Rocky knew he hadn't been mistaken.

Hmm. Interesting…

Not that he intended to explore any further than he had. Not that he thought she'd welcome it. "Smells good."

"Sit down. I didn't ask, but if you have a cholesterol problem, I have dry cereal."

"No problem." The table was set with the same old-fashioned dishes that clashed wildly with the yellow table. There was a toaster at one end, plastic place mats and paper napkins. On a shelf between two tall, narrow windows there was an overgrown vine in a jar and a few toothpicks in a hot-pepper-sauce bottle. He had a feeling both had been there long before Sarah took possession of her great-aunt's house.

Oddly enough, the place seemed to suit her, yet he knew for a fact that she'd been a privileged kid—in some ways. Needy as hell in others.

"If you've got a ladder, I can trade you a few

chores for last night's supper and this." He indicated the bacon and scrambled eggs she was dishing up.

"There's one in the shed. I fell off it and sprained my little finger last month trying to nail one of my shutters to the wall."

Sarah looked up in time to see the expression of—well, of something or other, on his face. "I know, I know, Grace is not my middle name."

"Your little finger?" He was grinning openly now. The voltage in a pair of pale-gray eyes set in a tanned, angular face, was potent enough to jumpstart a battleship. Heaven help any woman who got too close.

"I think I must have hit it on something coming down." She had to share his amusement. It was the one thing about her that no amount of ballet lessons and deportment classes had ever been able to remedy. "It's not that I'm uncoordinated so much as that my mind's usually on other things. I forget to watch where I'm going."

"Here's another hint for your survival guide. Whenever you're more than three feet off the ground, make certain your mind's on what you're doing."

"I landed in pine straw."

"Congratulations. We'll make a stunt woman out of you yet."

He dropped two slices of whole wheat into the toaster and opened a jar of Aunt Emma's homemade chunky apple preserves. "You do know your shutter's still dangling, don't you?"

"The hinges are so rusted I couldn't get the screws out."

"So you were going to what—nail it to the wall?"

"At least it would keep it from banging whenever the wind shifts."

"What about the BB hole?"

"In the window, you mean? Clear tape."

"Aha. There speaks a truly resourceful woman." He handed her a slice of toast, buttered and spread with preserves.

Rocky watched as she took a big bite and chewed thoughtfully. "I know," she said calmly after she'd swallowed. "At least, I'm finding out."

"What it is you're finding out?"

"How resourceful I am. Who I am. Who I want to be when I grow up. If I even want to grow up."

"Sounds like we've got us a mutual midlife crisis here. You want to join me in Never-Never Land?"

She laughed, and then he did, too, and when he complimented her on her cooking, she looked delightfully confused. "Well, I haven't had a whole lot to do lately but learn new things. Addie, our housekeeper, always did the cooking when I was growing up. Stan liked to eat out, and he never ate breakfast, anyway, even when he was home."

Back to ground zero. The wreckage of her marriage. Neither of them was ready to go there.

Nothing was said about his getting an early start. By late afternoon, after driving to Elizabeth City for hardware and making a couple of impulse buys while he was there, Rocky had replaced the windowpane and the rusted hinges on the west side of the house. There was a lot more that needed doing, but he reminded himself that her house was not his responsibility. He was merely earning his bed and board.

"I can't thank you enough," she said, standing on the ground and squinting up at the newly repaired blind. She was wearing jeans that looked as if they'd been left over from a sixties protest march. Maybe a protest of her own, he thought, amused.

"And for handling those reporters yesterday," she added earnestly.

"No problem. Small-time stringers. I doubt if they'll bother you again."

"Um...I don't remember seeing you at any of the hearings."

It was the first time they'd been mentioned directly. "I was mostly out of the country," he said, hoping she'd let it drop. He hadn't covered them personally, but he'd seen and heard enough. More than enough. On his frequent trips back to the States he'd been invited to air his opinion on a few Sunday-morning talk shows. He had declined. Media circuses left him cold, this one colder than most.

Except for the woman herself. There was a connection here that didn't make sense, but he'd learned never to dismiss his instincts. "Sarah, why do I get the feeling there's something you're not telling me?"

For a split second he thought he'd struck pay dirt, but she was no novice. "Not telling you? I thought anyone with a computer had instant access to everything about everybody. Let's see, now—age? Thirty-seven. Just last week, in fact. Weight? Somewhere between 110 and 117, depending on whether or not I remember to cut down on my salt intake. This is my real hair color and the only silicon on me is what I bring in on my shoes."

She was playing games. He recognized the ploy, but decided to let her run with it.

"I had an A-minus average through the first three years of college, but then it dropped to a C."

That would have been about the time she started seeing Sullivan.

"I like old-time fiddle music and opera, as long as I don't know the story and can make up my own to fit the music. I can play the harmonica pretty well—used to be able to, at least. I haven't tried in years."

He was grinning openly by now. She was a piece of work, all right. Great at playing defense, even if her only defense was facetiousness. Let's see how good she was at playing offense.

He gave her one she could hit out of the park. "I seem to remember reading that you did a lot of work with underprivileged children. Any ideas of looking for work in that area...when you're ready to move on, that is?"

"Do you want some coffee? There's about one cup left in the pot—I could add milk and ice it for you."

Struck out on an easy pitch. The fact that she hadn't even fanned it had to mean something. So now he knew where to start digging.

The trouble was, Sarah thought late that afternoon, that she enjoyed his company far too much. She had no business enjoying any man's company, much less that of a reporter. Or a journalist or a columnist or whatever you called a former political pundit who wasn't actively pursuing his career.

Of course, she only had his word that he wasn't.

What would he say if she told him about Kitty?

Would his first thought be the story, or the child's well-being? Would he think she was crazy for caring so much about a child she'd never even seen? One that proved beyond a doubt that her husband had been unfaithful?

For the sake of Kitty's future peace of mind, she couldn't take the risk. God knows what the Poughs would tell the child when she was old enough to ask about her father....

He was a kind, handsome man with a brilliant future, but unfortunately, darling, he died when you were too young to remember him.

For one brief moment Sarah wondered what Rocky would say if she told him the whole story—about the payments that were beginning to strain her modest resources. And the calls, always wanting to know if she couldn't send more. She was so afraid that if they kept on demanding more, and she kept insisting she couldn't send any more, they might go public. Not knowing what else to do, she'd taken to not answering her phone.

And on top of that, there was Clive and her father. Lord knows what those two wanted from her; she was afraid even to guess. Until she could come up with a good response, she preferred not to hear anyone's demands.

But, oh, how she wished she could walk into Rocky's arms, close her eyes and let the world disappear for one moment. He was the kind of man any woman would turn to instinctively in times of crisis, not because he had all the answers—or even a single answer—but because there were times when a woman simply needed to be held. No questions asked, no answers required—just the luxury of nonjudgmental physical comfort.

Sooner or later—probably sooner—she would have to leave here and find herself a job. Unless you were a farmer, there was no work to be had in Snowden. According to Aunt Emma, when the postmistress had retired before Sarah had even been born, there'd been no one under sixty-five to take her place, and so Snowden had lost its post office.

So maybe she could become a postmistress.

And go through a civil service exam?

No, thanks. There had to be a better way.

Rocky was on the ladder replacing the hinges on the east side of the house. For a reporter, he was surprisingly practical. It had never even occurred to her to plan her outside work around whichever side of the house the sun happened to be on. All afternoon she'd struggled under a blazing sun to pull down the rest of the grapevines.

"Why not use a weed killer, wait until they turn brown, then get rid of them once and for all?" He'd come up behind her so quietly she hadn't heard him.

Sweat dripping off the tip of her nose, she replied irritably, "Well, I guess it just never occurred to me."

Reaching past her, he grabbed a double handful of vine and pulled. Sarah turned and added her weight to the task, and suddenly, the huge, entangled vine gave way. Sarah staggered back.

Laughing, Rocky caught her before she could fall. "Easy there, we don't want anything else sprained, broken or bruised."

"Believe it or not," she said, hastily removing herself from his arms, "I've never broken a single bone."

"Then don't start by breaking one of mine."

She was still standing so close she could feel the heat of his body—smell the healthy male sweat. *Move, Sarah, move!*

"Don't move," he murmured. They were mere inches apart. With one hand he reached toward her hair. As his face came closer she could see the splinters of gold in eyes she had thought were pure silver. Her own eyes closed. Her lips softened expectantly.

"Gotcha!" He exclaimed triumphantly as he tugged at a handful of her hair.

Sarah slapped at his hand, feeling utterly mortified at what she'd been thinking. Expecting.

Oh, all right, *wanting!*

Glaring at the tiny worm he held dangling from a web between his fingers, she shuddered and started to back away.

Rocky caught her by the shoulders. "Whoa, not yet," he said softly. "There's something else we need to take care of."

And heaven help her, she stood there, dumb as a post, and lifted her face yet again.

Six

If she'd had an analytical mind, Sarah might have wondered how being kissed by one particular man could be so different from any other man in the world. Not that she'd kissed all that many men, but Rocky certainly wasn't the first. She'd been married, for heaven's sake! Why was her belly doing flip-flops, her pulse going haywire, just because she was being kissed for the first time in ages? The romance setting?

Hardly. Here she was, wearing her rattiest yard-working clothes, on the hottest day of the summer, knee-deep in a dusty tangle of wild grapevines—with a full-blown shiner, of all things—thinking thoughts she'd almost forgotten how to think!

Even the feel of his bristly jaw against her sun-flushed skin sent tingles all through her body. The feel of her nipples beading against her bra was almost painful. Wrapping her arms around his neck, she clung, savoring the moment. The thrill of his hard male body against hers. The way he tasted, the clean, fresh scent of his skin, his shirt.

You are so pathetic, *Sarah Mariah! Are you so starved for romance that you're turned on by* laundry soap?

Obviously she was.

When his lips finally left hers and he pressed her face against his shoulder, she breathed in deeply, waiting for the symptoms to fade. Was that his thudding heart or hers? His raspy, uneven breathing or hers? It had been so long....

Bitter memories raced back to haunt her. Stan had wanted to make love to her that last night. For the sake of appearances, they had stayed together during the trial. He'd been so distraught, so fragile, she'd been afraid of what he might do if she left him then. After weeks of coexisting in virtual silence while she'd made arrangements to sell the house and file for separation, he had come to her room one night and begged her to forgive him, to let them be together again. Knowing all she'd known by then, she couldn't bear for him to touch her, much less...*that.*

He'd gone down on his knees beside her bed and, with his arms around her waist, he had lowered his head to her lap and sobbed about how he'd been lured into the wild parties.

It had all started so innocently. First, drinks with a few big supporters. Then dinner with a small group of influential activists. After that, he'd been invited to a private party at the Georgetown home of a big contributor. Strictly stag. Not the sort of party a man invited his wife to attend, someone had joked.

There'd been party girls. It had never occurred to him that a few of them might have been underage. None of it had been his fault—someone must have put something in his drink, he'd claimed tearfully. He had sworn over and over that he was sorry, so very sorry—that he'd learned his lesson and it would never happen again.

It hadn't. He'd been killed the very next night. The unofficial verdict had been suicide. Since then Sarah had borne her own share of guilt, telling herself that if she hadn't been so unforgiving—if she'd somehow been a better wife in the first place, it would never have happened.

Now, lost in an unwanted rush of memories, she must have sighed, because Rocky stepped away, his hands still on her shoulders. "I'm fresh out of apologies. If you want me to leave, just say so."

She should. Not because of what had just happened, because she'd all but begged him to kiss her. But because he was a dangerous stranger, and she obviously wasn't quite as intelligent and independent as she'd hoped.

And because her face was throbbing again, and she was in no condition to deal rationally with any man, much less one who had such a powerful effect on her brain, not to mention her hormones.

"Could we please just not talk about it?" All right, so she was also a coward.

His gaze moved over her, making her painfully aware that not only was her face a mess, but she was wearing a T-shirt that dated from her college days and jeans she'd bought at a thrift shop—that her hair hadn't seen a stylist in more than a year, that it was tangled, decorated with twigs, pine straw and all manner of insects.

Nodding briefly, he said, "Sure. Why don't I finish the blinds while you catch your breath? You might want to put something on those scratches."

"Why don't you let me decide what I'm going to do?" she snapped.

So much for thirty-seven years of decorous behavior. *Will the real Sarah Mariah please stand up?*

Without another word, Rocky turned and headed for the shed. Sarah glared at his backside, the wide shoulders in a sweat-stained shirt, tapering down to a pair of narrow hips that were faithfully delineated by a pair of butt-worn jeans. Why was it that when men dressed in work clothes and got all hot and sweaty they looked perfectly delicious, while women just looked hot and sweaty?

If some self-appointed Sir Galahad insisted on riding to the rescue, why did it have to be the one man in all the world—well, other than Clint Eastwood— that she'd ever fantasized about?

Rocky swore under his breath. What the devil was he doing hanging around so long, anyway? So much for his noble intentions. The damned woman had taken advantage of him. She had no business looking at him that way, like she might wither and die if she didn't get kissed.

What was a guy supposed to do? He didn't want to hurt her feelings. And kissing her—well, black eye or not, it wasn't exactly a chore.

Okay, so he might have thought about it a few

times. Might even have wondered what she'd be like in bed—whether those decorous manners she'd practiced all her life would be in force behind closed doors. If she'd be wild and uninhibited in bed—or funny and sweet and klutzy.

Whatever else she was, she was an attractive woman, and he was a normal guy. The fact that he hadn't been with a woman sexually in a few years had nothing to do with it. He would never use Sarah that way.

Over the years there had been a few brief liaisons of a strictly physical nature. Nothing even faintly meaningful, because in spite of everything, he had never ceased to feel married. Which meant that whatever release he'd managed to find had been mixed up in his mind with guilt.

Hell of a thing, lusting after a woman he was trying to protect. Maybe they were both carrying too much baggage. He had come here with the best intentions in the world, but somewhere along the line he'd managed to misplace his objectivity. It wasn't the first time that had happened, which was one of the reasons he'd decided to hand in his resignation. Years of emotional exhaustion didn't leave a man much to work with.

Propping the ladder against the side of the house, he jabbed the feet into the ground to secure it and was halfway to the top before he remembered that he'd left his tools on the ground.

Oh, yeah, he was losing it, all right.

By the time he finished replacing the hinges and the hooks and eyes that held the shutters back against the wall, Rocky had managed to rationalize the situation to his own satisfaction.

With the old scandals about to be revived, even briefly, Sarah was the logical target of speculation. The basic story—the what, who, where and when—had long since been hashed out in public. With the chief perpetrator gone, the only remaining mystery was what had happened to the victim. In this case, the perp's widow. Where was she? Had she remarried? Taken lovers? Adopted her late husband's lifestyle? Would she turn up gracing the centerfold of some slick men's magazine?

Rocky had a feeling Sarah Mariah wouldn't like being considered a victim any more than she would like being tarred with the same brush as either of the two men in her life. As the self-designated good guy, he was in a position to ensure that that didn't happen. Or at least that she didn't suffer any personal embarrassment. And since he was already on the scene, he might as well hang around a few more days until things settled down. It wasn't as if there were any great demands on his time. He'd been in what was technically known as a deep blue funk for the past six months. This just might be the handle he needed to pull himself out.

The fact that they happened to find each other sexually attractive shouldn't be a problem, now that it had been brought into the open and acknowledged. They were both old enough to handle a mature, platonic relationship. With her quirky mind and his inquiring one, they could surely find ways of passing the time without getting into trouble until the hue and cry wore off and it was safe for him to leave. His stated plan of spending a night, then touring the area, had been mutually disregarded.

The phone was ringing some half hour later when he went back inside. Sarah had dragged the vines over to the side of the yard, left them there and was evidently upstairs showering. Rocky answered on the fourth ring.

"Sullivan residence."

Long pause. "Who the devil are you?"

"Friend of the family."

"Put my daughter on."

Rocky would have recognized the arrogance even if the man hadn't identified himself as Sarah's father. "She can't take a call at the moment, but I'll have her get back to you as soon as she's available." Grinning, he hung up on J. Abernathy Jones's squawk of protest.

And then he headed upstairs and rapped on the bathroom door. Hearing the sound of the shower cut off, he said, "Sarah? Call your dad."

Before he could turn away the door opened a crack. Sarah's face, purple shiner and all, emerged in a cloud of scented steam. "Call *who?*"

"The senator."

She started to shut the door, then opened it again. So far as he could tell—which wasn't far, just a glimpse of wet, gleaming shoulder—she didn't have on a stitch of clothing. "Did he say what he wanted?"

"Now, what do you think he wanted?" Might as well play a little devil's advocate as long as he was enjoying the view. Another day and her shiner would reach the apogee and start to fade. He figured the yellow-green stage might take another week, give or take, depending on how quickly she healed.

She chewed on her lower lip, and he was tempted

to say, If it needs chewing, let a real man tackle the job.

"I'm thirty-seven years old, for heaven's sake. I don't have to report to my father."

She looked wet and worried and funny and sexy, a dangerous combination. Rocky tried to ignore his body's eager response. "Shall I pass on the message when he calls back?"

"No, I—would you mind looking behind my bedroom door and handing me my robe? I was in such a hurry to scrub off any ticks and redbugs I forgot."

Glad of a mission—any mission—he turned away. Her room was at the opposite end of the hall from his, but it was a short hallway. Overcoming a reporter's natural curiosity, he located the cotton robe on a hook behind the door. In one sweeping glance, he took in the plain white cotton curtains, the plain white spread on the painted iron bed—and the desk. A guy could hardly be blamed for possessing finely honed powers of observation. It was an occupational hazard.

Mentally he filed away the details—the portable typewriter, the jar of ballpoints, another jar of paintbrushes and colored pencils. Feeling noble, he resisted the impulse to glance through the untidy stack of papers beside the manual typewriter and headed back to the bathroom, carrying the blue-flowered bathrobe.

He rapped on the door and held it out. "Any message in case he calls before you come downstairs?"

Sarah's hand, displaying a freshly applied assortment of strip bandages, reached through the door and took the robe. "Tell him—tell him I'm fine and I'll talk to him in a few weeks."

"Right."

"No, better yet, how about taking the phone off the hook?"

"Sarah, if you've got a problem with your old man, you can handle it yourself. Protecting ladies from the gutter press is one thing. Refereeing a father-daughter match is something else."

The bathroom door swung wide. She had toweled her hair until it stood out around her face in a wild tangle and tugged the robe on over a still-damp body. Later he told himself it was the look of her, all steamy and untidy, with that glorious purple shiner, that short-circuited his brain, allowing impulse to override intellect. Hands braced on the door frame, he leaned forward and touched her lips with his.

Funny thing—*scary* thing—somewhere in the back of his mind Rocky sensed that the kiss was only partly sexual. There was something more involved....

At the moment, however, he wasn't feeling particularly analytical. He knew only that he could no more resist kissing her than he could resist the laws of gravity.

"Well," she breathed long moments later, backing away to stare at him through the open bathroom door.

"My thoughts exactly," he said, which was an outright lie. If she knew what he was thinking, she'd be out of there like a shot, bare feet, wet hair and all.

Because once again he was wondering what she'd be like in bed. Like interference from a distant radio station, the thought kept intruding on his best intentions. There was a basic honesty about her that was enormously appealing, and that was the scary part. There was just too damn much about the woman that appealed to him.

Before he could make another mistake, he left. He was halfway down the stairs when he heard the bathroom door close. *Get it in gear, Waters. You've got a brain—use it!*

There was only one telephone in the house, an old rotary dial model. He could understand why someone might not want to be all that accessible. There'd been times over the past few years when he'd wanted to shout to the world, "Just leave me the hell alone!"

But for a woman living alone in the middle of a cornfield surrounded by forest, with the roof of the nearest neighbor barely visible, it was a different matter. What if she fell and hurt herself? With Sarah, that was a distinct possibility.

What if she had prowlers?

A cell phone would be the quickest fix, but only if she would remember to keep it close by. On second thought, maybe extensions in the kitchen, bathroom and bedroom would be the way to go. He could see to having the jacks installed before he left. He'd known a few people who were intimidated by cell phones. Sarah didn't strike him as a technophobe, but then, who else would use a manual portable typewriter when everyone else in the civilized world used a computer?

When he pictured the stack of papers on her desk, a sliver of curiosity flashed through his mind. He promptly stamped it out. *Not your business, Waters.*

Maybe she actually was working on the survival guide she'd mentioned. He'd thought she was joking at the time, but the more he thought about it, the more plausible it sounded. The lady had survived some pretty nasty stuff, and evidently she'd done it her way.

Maybe he could add a couple of chapters, himself. How to survive marriage without a wife? He had eventually found closure—peace, of a sort, but it hadn't been easy.

As for how to survive cynicism, the loss of ideals and the gradual disintegration of a career, he was still working on that chapter in his life. At the moment he didn't have a single opinion on politics, issues of national significance or world affairs that couldn't be summed up in a classified ad.

Oh, yeah…they were a pair, all right.

After leaving the hardware store in Elizabeth City that morning he'd located a newsstand and bought a selection of papers. Now he picked up the *Virginian-Pilot* and skimmed the headlines above the fold. Next he turned to the sports section and was about to settle down and catch up on the Braves' series when the phone rang again.

"I'm not in," Sarah called from upstairs.

"You're asking me to lie for you?" Tipping back his chair, he could see her at the head of the stairs. Dressed in more respectable white jeans and a baggy green T-shirt, she was worrying her lower lip again.

"I probably shouldn't ask you to do that. I'm sorry."

"Moot point. Whoever was on the other end just gave up."

Slowly she came down the stairs. She was barefoot. She had elegant feet—long, narrow and shapely, with pale, unpolished nails. It occurred to Rocky, not for the first time, that a brain could atrophy from lack of exercise.

"I guess it was the senator again."

She called him the senator. Not Father, not Dad or Daddy. It was a small thing but telling. He stood, waited for her to sit, and when she wandered over to the front window instead, he picked up the sports page again. Halfway through a piece on National League pitchers, he gave up and went back outside.

Even silent and still as a marble statue, the lady made waves.

It was late that afternoon when a car negotiated the crooked, rutted lane and pulled up in front of the house. Rocky was on the front porch fastening down the swollen board Sarah had been trying without success to repair. He stood and called quietly through the door, "Sarah, looks like you've got more company."

"Can you get rid of whoever it is?" He'd left her defrosting the old refrigerator. Messy job, but at least it was one she could probably handle without coming to too much grief.

"You might want to come outside. I don't think it's more reporters this time."

The driver got out and opened the back door of the black, late-model luxury sedan. Half expecting to see J. Abernathy emerge, it took Rocky several moments to identify the elderly man who stepped out. R. C. Detweiller, top aide and general dogsbody to the senator.

He stood and waited for the man to approach. "Detweiller," he said noncommittally. He'd met the man on several occasions. When there was no response, he introduced himself. "Rocky Waters. Formerly with Graves Worldwide and CCB, currently unaffiliated."

He stuck to the literal truth in case the man had a retentive memory.

"Waters." The desiccated individual wearing a three-piece suit on the hottest day in August looked as if had just smelled something unpleasant. "Is Mrs. Sullivan here?"

"I'm here, R.C." Sarah spoke from behind him, then stepped out onto the porch. She didn't invite him inside, even though Detweiller clearly looked as if he'd expected her to. She waved to the driver and called out, "Hi, Ollie. You're looking fit."

To Detweiller she said, "You might as well go back and tell my father I'm fine, I don't need anything from him, and if I ever do, I'll be sure to call."

Sarah hated having to air her personal affairs in public, but she wasn't about to let her father's right-hand man get a foot inside her door. He'd go back and describe every detail, right down to the puddle of melting ice on the kitchen floor. He was staring now in horror at her black eye. "Sarah Mariah, you haven't forgotten that your father's birthday is coming up, have you?"

Seven

"**Y**ou're asking for trouble," Rocky said quietly as they stood together on the front porch and watched the dusty black luxury sedan turn off the lane onto the dirt road.

"I don't have to ask, trouble always seems to find me."

"Want to go shopping for a birthday card?"

She offered him a wintry smile.

"Sarah, sooner or later you're going to have to deal with the man. He's your father, whatever else he is."

"Do you know, I used to wonder about that? We're nothing at all alike," she mused. "I didn't notice so much before Mama died, but after that... Well, of course I was too old for the usual fantasies—you know, being left on a doorstep or being the secret child of foreign royalty. But I did think maybe I might've been one of those—you know, donor babies? Um—artificial insemination?'' She slapped a hand over her face and groaned. "Why am I telling you all this?"

"Because the man who raised you as his daughter, whether it was technically true or not, is old and having a birthday and you're his only child. You're trying to talk your way out of a few perfectly natural guilt feelings."

"Are all reporters as irritating as you are?"

"We're a pretty shabby bunch, all right." Her elbow was there, right beside him, so he hooked his arm through the crook and tugged her against his side. "Ever look at the senator's eyes?"

She frowned up at him but didn't pull away. So he said, "Same mixture of gold, gray, green and brown."

She made a rude noise. "So? Billions of people have hazel eyes."

"Large, slightly tilted, set under perfectly arched brows. Of course, the senator's eyes are pretty well hidden by now unless he's had plastic surgery since I last saw him."

"Oh, I know he's my real father. I never actually doubted it, not down deep. Mama would have told me if there'd been anything—irregular. About me, I mean. My birth."

"How old is he? He's looked about the same age for as long as I can remember."

"Seventy-seven. I think. It's the hair. I'm not sure, but I think he might have had it bleached white when it started to go gray, and I do know he had at least one face-lift. He was supposed to be on an extended foreign trade thing. He is so vain."

Rocky considered reminding her of her filial obligation again, but it wasn't his place. Besides, in light of what the old pirate had put her through—put his entire constituency through, not to mention his country—he didn't deserve a dutiful daughter.

"We've never been big on birthdays. When I was little, Mama used to take me and my two best friends to the zoo and then out for burgers and cake. The year before she died—the year I turned thirteen—she treated us to makeovers. Professional manicures, hairstyles, makeup—the works. We giggled the whole time, and felt oh, so grown-up. Then we went home and stayed up all night watching videos and pigging out on pizza and milk shakes and birthday cake. Of course, the senator had no part in any of these birthday bashes. Mama used to sign his name to whatever gift she gave me, but he couldn't have cared less. Birthdays never interested him, unless it was someone important."

The implication being that she wasn't. Why wasn't he surprised?

The phone rang before the dust had settled out on the road. Evidently R.C. had lost no time in getting back to his employer. After five rings Sarah muttered something surprisingly profane and stalked inside, slamming the door behind her.

"All right, all right," she practically shouted into the receiver. She knew the routine. First her father would send one of his minions to soften her up, then he'd try another tactic. This time he'd called personally, sent in the troops when she refused to answer, and now that he thought he'd softened her up sufficiently, he was going to try again.

"Sarah Mariah?" When had he begun to sound so old? He'd always used his syrupy baritone voice the

way he used his silver hair, his courtly mannerisms—
even his family. To create an impression. Now his
voice sounded querulous, and he had no family left.
Only Sarah.

She tried not to feel guilty, but only partly succeeded. ''Yes, Father.'' Closing her eyes, she took a
deep breath. Damn him—damn the whole Washington
mess—she hadn't been able to work on Kitty's story
in days. She had finished the drawings, but she hadn't
had time to finish the story.

''I'm having a small celebration next week and I
want you to come home.''

''Happy birthday, Father. I am home.'' She wasn't
about to give an inch. She knew him too well. At the
first sign of weakness, the battle was over. She had
lost too many times ever to surrender without putting
up a fight.

''It'll be a quiet celebration, naturally. I'm afraid
I'm not up to anything more strenuous. Of course, if
your mother were still here, God rest her soul, it might
be a different matter. Having family around to brighten
the home gives a man strength.''

Since when? she wanted to ask. His voice actually
quavered. Sarah could picture him wiping away a tear
and hardened herself against being swayed. When bul-
lying failed, he played the obligation card. Piety was
the last resort, but there wasn't a pious bone in his
body, and they both knew it.

''The river house is your home, not mine, Father.
Why don't you invite a few friends to come fish and
play golf and cards with you? You really don't need
me.''

She didn't know what his household staff consisted

The Silhouette Reader Service™ — Here's how it works:

Accepting your 2 free books and gift places you under no obligation to buy anything. You may keep the books and gift and return the shipping statement marked "cancel." If you do not cancel, about a month later we'll send you 6 additional novels and bill you just $3.34 each in the U.S., or $3.74 each in Canada, plus 25¢ shipping and handling per book and applicable taxes if any.* That's the complete price and — compared to cover prices of $3.99 each in the U.S. and $4.50 each in Canada — it's quite a bargain! You may cancel at any time, but if you choose to continue, every month we'll send you 6 more books, which you may either purchase at the discount price or return to us and cancel your subscription.

*Terms and prices subject to change without notice. Sales tax applicable in N.Y. Canadian residents will be charged applicable provincial taxes and GST.

GET FREE BOOKS and a FREE GIFT
WHEN YOU PLAY THE...

Just scratch off the silver box with a coin. Then check below to see the gifts you get!

SLOT MACHINE GAME!

7	7	7	**Worth TWO FREE BOOKS plus a BONUS Mystery Gift!**
🎵	🍒	🍒	**Worth TWO FREE BOOKS!**
♣	♣	♣	**Worth ONE FREE BOOK!**
🔔	🔔	🍒	**TRY AGAIN!**

Visit us online at www.eHarlequin.com

DETACH AND MAIL CARD TODAY!

of now, or if he could even afford to hire anyone. She did know better than to let herself be talked into anything. He was good at it—he was superb—but she knew him too well.

Carefully, she hung up the phone on his arguments. She was still standing there, her back rigid with resentment, when Rocky came inside. At the same moment that she became aware of his presence behind her, she felt his hands close over her shoulders, warm and comforting. Instinctively she tipped her head back against his shoulder. If ever a woman needed a friend—a nonjudgmental friend—it was when guilt and doubts and fears were all mixed up in her mind with lust and curiosity and... "Aah," she whispered.

He began to knead the tense muscles. Neither of them spoke a word. Magic hands manipulated the knots in her shoulders, working their way toward her neck. His thumbs reached up and stroked the sides of her throat until she went limp, and then he pulled her back against him and held her there. Simply held her, his arms around her waist, her head tipped back on his shoulder, his cheek resting on her hair.

"How do you feel about seafood?" His raspy baritone reverberated all the way to the soles of her feet, and her mind raced back to their first meeting.

"Are we talking guppy filets?"

He laughed aloud then, his warm breath stirring through her hair. "Don't you ever forget anything?"

"Only important things. Trivia stays with me forever."

"Half an hour or so and we can be at the beach. Want to gamble on finding a vacant table?"

"Deal!" she crowed instantly.

* * *

Sarah couldn't believe how good it felt to get away. With the vacation crowd at its peak, she would be just one of the hoard. And if there happened to be a reporter around—other than Rocky, that was—he'd be far more interested in the sand-sculpture contests, surfing competitions and the hang gliders on Kill Devil Hills than in an almost-middle-aged widow who happened to be slightly connected to a couple of old scandals.

Say, aren't you congressman whatsisname's widow? What do you think of Ms. Cudahy's book? Have you read it yet? Are you going to sue the publisher?

It probably wouldn't be the first time the paparazzi had tried to stir up the coals of an old scandal when they ran out of fresh material. She hadn't read the damn book, didn't intend to and didn't want to hear another word about it. As for suing, what grounds did she have? There was no libel involved, so far as she knew. The whole mess might have died a natural death if Stan hadn't broken down in the most public place— the house floor, with the cameras rolling, no less—and confessed his part of the whole sordid affair.

Naturally the press had jumped on it like flies on roadkill, but in the end, not even confession and public humiliation had been enough to assuage his guilty conscience.

"How do you feel about raw bars?"

Glad of the diversion, she replied, "In a word? Yuk."

They were listening to one of Rocky's CDs, something smooth and heavy and vaguely familiar as they drove onto the Currituck Sound Bridge. He was humming along with the haunting refrain. Sarah would have figured him for soft rock or jazz. So much for her judgment.

They found a restaurant that looked well patronized without being too crowded. He pulled in, switched off the engine and turned to face her. "Look, if you change your mind at any time, we can just get up and walk out, okay? If you feel the least bit uncomfortable, just say the word."

"Oh, for heaven's sake, it's not like I was a celebrity or anything. I doubt if one out of ten million people even know I exist. We're not in Washington now, or even Virginia or Maryland."

"We're not in Kansas now, Toto," he said with a lopsided grin. "Point taken."

Once inside, he drew the hostess aside and spoke a few quiet words. The stylish middle-aged woman palmed the bill, and after one quick glance at Sarah's glorious shiner, which no amount of makeup would completely disguise, led them over to a candlelit table for two overlooking the ocean.

"Oh, this is wonderful! And we didn't even have reservations, can you believe our luck?" Wearing a sleeveless ankle-length cotton dress in a splashy red-and-white print she managed to look cool, sophisticated, yet very much like a kid on Christmas morning. Watching her face glow with excitement, Rocky reminded himself that this was a woman who'd been holed up alone in the middle of a cornfield for nearly a year. Given another few weeks, she might even have welcomed the press.

"This is great, it's just perfect!" she whispered. Leaning over, she peered out the window, watching a lazy surf lap the flat, sandy shore. "I must say, you do have the most marvelous ideas!"

For the next few minutes Sarah studied the menu while Rocky studied the woman.

Odd, the way different women could affect a man. Feature by feature she was nothing out of the ordinary. Yet, even with a few minor flaws—such as the black eye and half a dozen or so awkwardly placed cowlicks—she struck him as one of the loveliest women he'd ever met.

It had been Julie's looks he'd noticed first. Any man would. She could have made it as a model, easily, if she hadn't been more interested in getting her degree. They'd both wanted kids, Julie because she'd come from a large family, he because he'd come from a long line of foster homes. They'd planned to wait a few years, find an affordable place in the country to raise a family—and then suddenly it was too late.

Too late...

"Do you mind if I order the seafood platter and don't eat everything? I hate waste. My great-aunt— the one who gave me her house? She always used to say, 'Remember the poor starving children,' when I didn't clean off my plate, but I hate to eat too much."

"My wife would have liked your great-aunt."

And there it was. "Your...wife?"

"Her name was Julie. She died this past February after a long illness." It was all he intended to say. Hadn't intended to say that much, but suddenly he'd heard himself bringing Julie into the conversation, as if she'd needed to be there.

Sarah reached across the table and covered his hand with hers. "I'm sorry."

Those expressive eyes of hers said more than her words. He nodded and glanced down at his menu, forestalling questions he wasn't ready to hear, much less try to answer. It might have been easier if he'd been indifferent to her. Unfortunately, he was attracted not only to her body, but to her mind. Lust and like were a volatile combination.

On assignment in a war-ravaged country a few years ago he'd had to make his way through a minefield. What he was feeling now differed only in degree. Closing a door in his mind, he smiled across the table. "Why don't we order a selection of appetizers and then share a seafood platter?"

If there was a hidden analogy there, he was pretty sure it escaped her. Actually, there wasn't. At least, not intentionally.

"If we overdo it, we'll head for the beach and walk it off." He regretted the offer as soon as the words were spoken. *What the devil were you thinking about, Waters? A moonlight stroll on the beach with a beautiful woman?*

Well, hell—he could hardly rush her through dinner, then race back to Snowden, dump her out and hightail it back to his empty apartment in Chevy Chase.

She nodded, her smile just a little more guarded, a little less eager than it had been only moments ago. Which made him feel churlish. It was hardly her fault that something inside him that had been frozen for nearly seven years was beginning to thaw. Or that the thawing process was so painful.

They ate a variety of seafood, boiled, broiled and fried. They drank wine, probably a mistake, but the sound of Sarah's laughter as the meal progressed was enough to make up for any reservations he might have had. A long, leisurely walk on the beach with the wind blowing in his face should take care of any residual effects before they headed home. So what if he was rationalizing? As for the slight buzz he was feeling now, Sarah's laughter was more than enough to maintain that.

The tide was out, the beach flat and surprisingly uncrowded—perfect for walking. Arm in arm, carrying their shoes, they walked silently for the first few hundred feet, then paused to watch the moon emerging from the black waters of the Atlantic. Sarah told herself that someday she was going to show Kitty this same moon and the path it made, like a magic golden highway.

Holding hands, they talked very little, each content to absorb the beauty and peace of the moment. It was an oddly satisfying silence. Surprisingly comfortable. Reaching a place where erosion had narrowed the beach so that they would have had to pick their way past obstacles—parts of a boardwalk and the foundation of a cottage—Rocky paused, nodded back toward the way they had come. Without a word they turned, both smiling but silent, as if recognizing that as long as they didn't allow the real world to intrude, they were safe.

Then Sarah, still watching the rising moon, caught her foot on something half-buried in the sand and would have fallen if Rocky hadn't held on to her. Embarrassed, she allowed him to dust the sand off her foot and examine it for damage. "You think I'm a klutz, don't you? Well, I'm really not. Sometimes I just don't notice things when I'm thinking about something else."

"The old absentminded professor defense. Oh, yeah, I've heard that one before. So what lofty thoughts were you thinking that caused you to trip over a fully visible eight-by-eight timber?"

"If you really what to know, I was picturing a tiny yellow boat sailing off along a streak of yellow moonlight with a little yellow-haired girl at the helm and wondering what color the life preservers would be."

He stared at her for a full ten seconds. "Uh-huh. That's what I thought you were thinking."

The moon was bright enough that Rocky could see her expression clearly. She looked like a kid who'd been caught sampling the frosting with a finger. "Sarah? Is there something you're not telling me?"

"Of course there is. What do you want to hear first, that two of my teeth are crowns? That in college I made it a policy to read every banned book I could get my hands on? That I wish I'd had room tonight to try that lime-fig cake? Or that wine always makes me sleepy, and I'm afraid I'll snore on the way home?"

"Sarah, Sarah, Sarah..." As a klutz she was appealing. As a belligerent klutz, she was purely irresistible.

Blame it on the wine—blame it on the moonlight— blame it on the woman. Before sanity could set in Rocky gathered her to him, anchored his feet in the sand and lowered his face to hers.

She tasted of coffee. Smelled of sea, Sarah and Shalimar. It was a heady combination. "Oh, Sarah,

Sarah, what am I going to do about you?" Rocky whispered against fragrant wisps of windblown hair. He was embarrassingly aroused, and there was no way he could disguise the fact.

As one, they moved higher on the beach, to the dune line. Sea oats brushed past as he lowered her carefully onto the dry sand, still warm from the day's sun, then came down beside her.

"Put your head on my arm," he said. "You'll get your hair full of sand."

"I don't mind, but I do hate sandy sheets. Maybe I can wear a hat to bed tonight."

Stroking her side, his hand moved over her hips, along her waist, to her arm and then her breast. Rocky chuckled softly, picturing her lying nude in her bed, wearing that hideous straw hat she claimed was her gardening hat but never wore.

"Any woman who can make a man laugh and make him want to jump her bones at the same time is more valuable than, uh—rubies and pearls."

"Did you just make that up or did you read it in a book somewhere?"

"What do you think?" His lips traced a path from her ear to the hollow at the base of her throat. He shifted her so that she was lying on top of him—the least he could do, since he hadn't thought to bring a blanket. It had never occurred to him because this shouldn't be happening. Neither of them was ready for it. "Nowhere near ready," he murmured as he captured the sandy back of her head and lowered her mouth to his.

If he were any more ready, he wouldn't be able to move. Making out on the beach like a horny adolescent? Getting turned on by a zany, klutzy, sexy woman at his age?

Her breasts were small. She wasn't wearing a bra. Panties and a dress. Total nudity couldn't have been any more arousing. Her nipples peaked against his palms, sending a message to his groin.

Slowly he withdrew his hands from under her dress. Her skin was gritty—so was his. Hardly optimum conditions for what this was leading up to. Clasping her face in his hands, he brushed his lips back and forth over hers, savoring the drag of moist softness.

"I guess this wasn't too smart," he said.

"I guess it wasn't," she agreed.

He could hear the rueful smile in her voice. "It's been a while since I've gone for a moonlight walk on a beach. I forgot to bring a blanket."

"Just as well. I never go to bed on a first date," she said, trying unsuccessfully to make light of what had just happened. What was still happening. She rolled off his body and sat up. Heels dug in, knees sprawled apart, she proceeded to brush the sand from her hair.

By the time they reached the parking lot and he helped her in, brushed off her feet and slid her sandals on, they had both more or less regained their composure.

More or less.

You're forty-four years old, man. A little restraint might be in order.

"I thought I might head back home tomorrow," he said as they rolled back onto the bridge. "We've probably seen the last of the tabloid press, and the legitimate guys aren't going to bother you."

''I expect you're right,'' she said quietly, and Rocky told himself it was only his imagination that she sounded...

Stricken.

Eight

After a restless night, not entirely due to the grit on her pillow, Sarah opened her eyes and lay there, wondering if it was too late to salvage her dignity. Watching patterns of sunlight dance across the ripples in old floral wallpaper, filtered through the pines outside, she went over all that had happened—or so nearly happened—on the beach last night.

The man had lost his wife less than a year ago, for heaven's sake!

And what had she done? She'd shamelessly tried to seduce him, that's what! Going without a bra, dabbing perfume in strategic places so that body heat would make it rise around her. Drinking wine. Laughing.

Oh, Lord, she hoped she hadn't actually batted her eyelashes at him. Under the circumstances that would have been truly grotesque.

As for the perfume, it was probably rancid, considering it was several years old. Stan had hated it, claiming it was too old-fashioned. He'd given her a huge bottle of one of those aggressive new fragrances, which had gone to Goodwill along with what she had thought of as her work costumes. The neat little outfits that were neither too smart nor too dowdy for a politician's wife, all totally without personality.

"Sarah? You awake?"

Great. The day was half over, he was going to leave—the coward—and she was lying in bed, wallowing in regrets, embarrassment and a dozen other nonproductive emotions.

"Be down in a minute!" She jumped out of bed and scrambled through her closet for something flattering to put on. "Forget flattering, settle for decent," she muttered.

She settled for clam diggers, clogs and a camp shirt, which she buttoned up wrong and then had to do over again. No time for makeup—she splashed her face, gargled and made a pass at her hair with a brush, all without confronting the mirror.

This was the end. He was leaving. It was probably for the best, she thought, but it might take a few years—a few decades—to convince herself.

"Sarah, get a move on, will you? We've got company again."

Company? "Oh, shoot." Dropping the brush, she clattered down the hall, down the stairs and out onto the porch just as a familiar silver car, the kind that reeked status, pulled up in front of the house.

Clive Meadows. Why the devil couldn't they take no for an answer?

Rocky had chosen to stay inside this time, which was just as well. The last thing she needed was to have to explain him to another of her father's emissaries. For some obscure reason the senator had been pushing her toward Clive—or him toward her—since practically the day after Stan had died.

Her shoulders sagged, but she managed to hold on to a smile as the dapper, gray-haired man stepped out of the driver's seat. *Shake every hand, kiss every baby and smile, smile, smile, no matter that your feet are killing you and you're coming down with cramps.* She'd done the drill a thousand times. "Clive, how lovely to see you."

Lovely didn't quite describe what she was feeling at the moment. She knew for a fact that he was sixty-nine. Thanks to a personal trainer and an excellent tailor, he looked at least ten years younger.

Halfway up the front walk, the lawyer-turned-lobbyist stopped and gaped at her face. At her eye. "My God, Sarah, what on earth happened to you? R.C. said—but I never expected— How did it happen?"

"I ran into a door, and don't you dare say one word about what a klutz I am." Clive had seen her at her worst—stepping off the edge of a stage as she tried to escape the mob congregating around her father—getting her bracelet caught in her hair while trying to adjust her hat at a state funeral. The more exhausted she was, the more accident-prone she became.

If her smile now was a little too bright, at least it served to deflect his attention from her eye. The swelling was down, but the ghastly blend of yellow, green and lavender was still visible. "Are you on your way to the beach, or on your way back home?"

She had stayed at his beach house several times, occasionally with Stan, more often with the senator. Clive Meadows was an excellent host who frequently entertained the rich and influential. Which was why, Stan had once told her, his palatial beach house was a total tax write-off. Stan had been pressing her for years to go shopping with him for a beach place of their own, when they could barely afford the payments on their modest six-room house.

"I was on my way down when it occurred to me that you might enjoy a break from..." His expression when he glanced at the surrounding cornfields spoke volumes. As skilled as he was at lying, Sarah easily detected her father's meddling hand. "It's sweet of you to offer, Clive, but as you can see, I'm right in the middle of a serious attack of landscaping." She gestured toward the mass of grapevines, honeysuckle and pruned branches he was being forced to negotiate to reach the porch.

Reaching her side, he kissed her lightly as he'd been doing for years. "How are you, my dear? Aside from the obvious, I mean. We've been worried, your father and I."

"I can't imagine why. I told the senator I was perfectly well. I love it here, I always have."

"I can see you've been working too hard. You really should hire someone to do that, Sarah Mariah. You deserve a long, restful weekend at the cottage. On Monday or Tuesday we can drive up the Eastern Shore, stop in at St. Michaels for lunch and still arrive in plenty of time for your father's birthday celebration.''

''No.''

Ignoring her—he was almost as good at doing that as the senator was—Clive went on to say, ''I met your great-aunt once. Lovely woman—lovely. But my dear, you can't hibernate forever. Now, what do you say to spending a quiet, relaxing few days soaking up sun— you can have the pool all to yourself, there's no one at the cottage but staff.''

She crossed her arms over her chest. Dammit, why did he insist on treating her as if she were a rebellious teenager? Was this the way he'd treated his wives? She knew for a fact that the last one had just turned twenty when they met. No wonder none of his marriages had lasted much longer than it took the ink to dry on the prenuptial agreements.

And another thing—it had always irritated her that he insisted on referring to his beach house as ''the cottage.'' Eight bedrooms and nine baths, including an outside shower and a full bath in the pool house, did *not* a cottage make! ''You're too generous, Clive, but—''

Behind her the screen door opened and closed quietly. ''What Sarah's trying to say, Meadows, is that she has a houseguest and she's far too conscientious a hostess to leave while I'm still here.''

Not by so much as a raised eyebrow did the older man show his surprise. But then, he must have known all along. That was probably why he was here. R.C. had gone back and told her father that Sarah had a man staying with her, and the senator had called in the heavy artillery.

Stiff-lipped with anger and frustration, Sarah introduced the two men. Clive said, "Waters," and extended his hand. He laid on what Sarah had always thought of as his snake-oil smile. She might like him, but that particular smile was one of the things that kept her from ever taking him at his word.

"We've met," said Rocky.

The lawyer nodded genially. "I don't recall seeing you around town lately. Rumor has it you've retired."

Sarah watched as they sized each other up like a couple of strange dogs, each trying to establish dominance. Although in Rocky's case, with his six feet plus of prime masculinity, no effort was required.

"Oh, for heaven's sake, as long as you're here, Clive, you might as well come inside for coffee. I haven't even had breakfast yet."

Rocky obviously had. His dishes were neatly stacked in the sink. She watched as Clive took in every single sign of intimacy, from the dishes in the sink to the moccasins Rocky wore when he was working around the house, which shared a mat with her mud shoes beside the back door. His Braves cap hung on a hook beside the straw hat she wore for yard work when she happened to remember to put it on.

"I'll make a fresh pot," Rocky said just as if it were his kitchen and Clive was his guest instead of hers. He was doing it deliberately, and for the life of her, Sarah couldn't imagine why he should want to complicate matters any more than they already were.

"Don't bother. On second thought," the lawyer said, "I'd better not stay long enough for coffee." His narrowed eyes hard as agates despite his surface geniality, he added, "*This* time."

Stepping back toward the door, he smiled at Sarah, nodded at Rocky and touched the side of the old walnut wag-tail clock that had hung there between the door and the china cabinet for as long as Sarah could remember. "Nice piece. Not really valuable, but... rather charming."

In other words, Rocky interpreted, *There's nothing of value here, Waters, so buzz off.* Instead of the simple infrared detector he'd bought and installed at the foot of the lane, he should have bought a Doberman with a taste for Washington lobbyists.

Rocky stayed inside while Sarah saw her guest on his way. In the process of making a fresh pot of coffee, he just happened to stroll into the front hall as she was walking the jerk to his car. They lingered to talk for several minutes. Then Meadows kissed her again. She turned her head just in time so that the kiss slid harmlessly off her cheek, but Rocky, watching through the screen door, felt something snap in his hand. Swearing softly, he retrieved the plastic handle of the coffee measurer he'd been holding.

"Sounds like a nice vacation," he said with deceptive mildness when she came back inside. "Why didn't you take him up on it? A whole swimming pool all to yourself?"

"Oh, shut up!"

Grinning, he used a damp paper towel to clean up the few grounds that had scattered on the floor when the measuring spoon had broken. "Yes, ma'am."

She turned and glared at him. "Well, what would you do in my place? I've known the man practically all my life. He's my father's best friend, his lawyer and God knows what else."

"I don't recall seeing him much during the Senate hearings."

She shrugged. "He hasn't actually practiced in years. Stan said he directed the entire defense from behind the scenes."

"In that case, why didn't he do a better job of it?"

Her arms flew out in a gesture of helpless frustration. "How do I know? Why don't you ask him, if you're so curious?"

"He did what he had to do, Sarah," Rocky said gently. "Your father was guilty as hell, and we both know it. At least he didn't have to serve any prison time."

"Oh, I know, I know. I'm just feeling..." She hugged her arms around her and stared out the kitchen window at the flock of crows squabbling in the pines on the far side of her cornfield.

"Trapped?" Rocky supplied.

Sarah nodded. She rarely cried. For one thing it never helped. For another, she didn't cry any more gracefully than she did anything else. Her eyes turned red, her nose stopped up, and nothing short of a tourniquet around her neck could silence her wails.

When the first sob escaped she muttered, "Hellfire and damnation," but the words were punctuated by a shuddering hiccup. Rocky's arms closed around her, and she gave in and buried her face against his shirt. The dam burst then, and it all came spilling out—anger, fear on behalf of an innocent child whose whole life might be shadowed by Stan's sins if the connection was ever made.

And grief because of something she was only now beginning to understand—that here was a man she could have loved—one who might even have loved her, if only they'd met at a different time, under different circumstances. It was like discovering the end of the rainbow just as the lights went out.

The more she tried to stifle her tears—to shove the evil genie back into the bottle—the more impossible it became, until she gave up trying. Better to get it out of her system and move beyond it.

He was good at holding, good at comforting, offering empathy, not pity. Finally, after one last shuddering sob, she sniffed. Rocky shoved a handkerchief into her hand. She mopped, blew and managed to get control of her breathing, but she refused to lift her head from his shoulder. "I never, *ever* do this," she told him. "You obviously bring out the worst in me."

"Funny you should say that. Now me, I've got a totally different take on it. Sit down while I pour the coffee and make you some toast and I'll enlighten you."

Well, what could she do? He'd already seen her at her worst. Her rock-bottom worst. And she was starving. A morning person, she always ate a substantial breakfast.

While she got herself under control, he made *huevos rancheros*. She hadn't had them since her Mexican honeymoon. She'd hated Cancun, but loved the food. Now she gobbled up half her huge serving before she dared lift her face to look at him. He was seated across the table, nursing a cup of rich black coffee.

"It's great. Thank you. I—" She started to say, she'd thought he was leaving, but changed direction just in time. "I wish we could get real Mexican coffee here."

"You can. It just doesn't taste the same unless it's made with Mexican water."

Which brought on a smile, a sigh and another flood of useless emotion. "Sorry about the histrionics. I don't usually lose control that way."

"I know."

Oblivious of her naked face, her reddened eyes and her fading bruises, she gave him a searching look. "You do?"

"Sarah, I watched most of the coverage these past few years. Both times. It was brutal—even though it was largely deserved in both cases. You stood up under pressure magnificently. I was proud of you."

"You were?"

God, would you look at her, Rocky marveled. How could any woman look so beautiful with a week-old shiner, tearstained cheeks, pink eyes and a red-tipped nose? It had to be that sweet, vulnerable mouth—either that or the wistful, hopeful expression. Whatever it was, he was a sucker for it.

And that was a damned shame, because he hadn't figured on getting personally involved here. He'd done his Don Quixote thing. Now, if he had a grain of sense, he'd saddle up the Rover and ride off into the sunset. Get the hell out of Dodge. He could think of a number of clichés that all meant the same thing. Get out before he got into more trouble than he'd bargained for.

The driveway alarm went off again, and Sarah jumped. "Oh, no," she wailed.

He'd bought it without asking permission when he'd bought the hinges and had finished installing it just yesterday. He'd had in mind nosy reporters, not rabbits, deer and whatever other creatures, two- or four-legged, might be prowling the countryside. In such an isolated setting, a woman living alone needed more security. At the very least, she needed a warning.

"Probably just a deer. Wait here, I'll check it out," he said, sliding his chair back.

A moment later he was back. "Did your friend leave something behind? He's headed this way again."

"Clive? Why on earth would he come back?"

"Maybe he just doesn't like taking no for an answer."

This time they were both waiting on the front porch when the car pulled into the yard. Clive Meadows got out, shut the door and paused as if collecting himself to present his closing statement.

Rocky beat him to the punch. "Forget something, Meadows?"

"I believe I might have done just that. Sarah, I didn't tell you the whole truth before. I wasn't sure how you'd take it."

"Now, why am I not surprised?" Rocky muttered.

Sarah said nothing, but when his hand brushed against hers, she grabbed it and held on.

"It's about your father. The senator."

"I know who my father is," she said, not yielding an inch.

Meadows stopped at the bottom of the painted concrete steps, one tasseled loafer propped on the first step. "He's...not well, Sarah Mariah. I don't know how much he's told you, but your father suffers from a heart condition."

Sarah's hand tightened convulsively. She took a

deep breath and then, in a controlled voice, asked, "How long?"

"How long does he have? Or how long has he known?"

"Both. Everything! Why wasn't I told before now? Is he—is he hospitalized? Has he had a heart attack?"

When Meadows moved up another step, Rocky decided it was time to take over. The guy had just invited her to the beach for a cozy weekend. Would he have done that if her father's condition was critical? Something wasn't right here. "Give us the name of the senator's cardiologist. We'll take it from there."

The lawyer stared at him as if he'd just crawled up out of the primordial slime. "I don't believe this involves you, Waters."

"As Sarah's fiancé, anything that involves her happiness involves me. Now, you want to give me the doctor's name and the name of the hospital?"

"Her fiancé?" The older man looked from one to the other, his disbelief plain to see. "Since when?"

Rocky's smile was a wicked work of art. "Under the circumstances, we decided to keep things pretty low-key. I'm sure you understand."

Sarah hadn't said a word. Evidently she'd already depleted her emotional reserves. Thank God for that. If she fell apart on him now, it would be just the tool this jerk needed.

So he said softly, not caring whether or not the other man could hear, "Sarah, I'm pretty sure the situation is under control, considering Meadows just invited you to a private pool party."

Releasing his hand, Sarah moved to the edge of the porch. "Well? What about that, Clive? If the senator is in such dire straits, why didn't you offer to take me to him instead of down to the beach for a vacation?''

Way to go, honey. Put him on the defensive.

"Well, naturally I intended to explain once we were alone and could talk privately.'' The man was a master at subtle intimidation, Rocky thought with reluctant admiration. Evidently, it came with the territory.

But Sarah wasn't too shabby herself when it came to sending the opposition scurrying. After a few more attempts to persuade her to go with him, the lawyer stalked off, slammed into his dusty silver chariot and roared off down the potholed lane.

That's my girl, Rocky thought proudly. Whatever she needed to know about the senator's health, they would find out together.

Nine

Clogs were good for stomping, and Sarah was in a stomping mood. She stomped into the kitchen, yanked open the refrigerator door looking for canned milk. Finding the can empty, she slammed the door and stomped across to the pantry.

"Do you know how frustrating it is when a woman can't even believe her own father? Why is it," she demanded plaintively, "that all the men in my life are such world-class liars?"

Fresh can in hand, she jerked open a drawer and found an opener. Evaporated milk spilled on the counter when she popped it open. "Crooked, self-serving, conniving—"

"Present company excluded, I hope," Rocky said, testing her with a bit of gentle teasing.

It took some of the wind out of her sails. "Don't

push me too far, Waters, I'm not in the mood.'' She poured herself a fresh cup of coffee and cursed the cretin who had designed a coffeepot with a leaky, inefficient spout.

Sarah Mariah was on a roll. Silently, Rocky blotted the spilled milk and mopped up the rich brown puddle with a handful of paper towels. If the conversation needed a nudge, he'd nudge. Right now what she needed was to blow off steam.

She was worried but afraid to admit it. Perfectly understandable, Rocky reasoned. Whatever else he was, the senator was her father. He also reasoned that if the situation had been critical, Meadows would have told her straight out.

Instead he'd invited her to his beach house.

Obviously, the snake was up to something, and whatever it was, J. Abernathy was probably in it with him, up to their collective necks. Rocky had a suspicion of what was going on; what he didn't understand was why.

Unless the senator owed Meadows big time, which was a distinct possibility—and he was using Sarah Mariah as bargaining chip. Also a possibility, considering the old pirate's history.

Viewing the situation from Meadows's point of view, it was a bit harder to figure. If his past wives were anything to go by, then Sarah was hardly his type. Only child of a dedicated socialite and a crooked politician, her entire life had been constrained, first by her parents and then by that idiot she'd had the misfortune to marry. In some ways she was remarkably naive. The one thing that could be said of all of Meadows's wives was that they were far from naive.

The trouble, Rocky told himself, with trying to second-guess this particular situation was that one of the suspects was a lawyer and the other had spent more than half his life in politics. In both cases the thought patterns were so labyrinthine, so convoluted, that every word, deed or motive was suspect.

"I'll have to go, you know." Sarah continued to spoon sugar into her cup as she stared through the window at a wren that was busy exploring a section of newly exposed gutter.

"You could call."

"I could, but if I'm to have the slightest chance of finding out the truth, I'll have to see him face-to-face."

No need to ask who "him" was. The first time he'd ever met her, she'd had much the same look about her. Resigned, but far too vulnerable. Back then he'd tried to tease her out of it. This time teasing wasn't going to work. He ached to hold her. Ached to do far more than hold her, but she was still too fragile. For a man who had come here with only the most altruistic intentions—well, perhaps he might have toyed briefly with the idea of writing her story himself—he had already strayed too far off course. For both their sakes he needed to take a giant step back and regain his objectivity.

"When?" he asked, masking his concern.

She stared at her oversweetened coffee in disgust and poured it in the sink. "Today—no, tomorrow. I'll need to close up the house, stop the paper delivery, pack a few things—enough for two or three days, I guess. Lord only knows..." Her voice trailed off as she went off into what he'd taken to calling her mini-trances.

He broke into her concentration. "I can close up the house for you, turn everything off and leave the key where you can find it when and if you come back."

"When, not if." There was a glittery look to her eyes that might be tears, but this time he didn't think so.

And then it dawned on him that the lady wasn't worried. What she was, was mad as hell. Rocky was amused. Amused, but no less concerned. "It's the Wye River place, right? You want company? It's not all that far out of my way."

"No, I..." She slapped her hand to her forehead, as if she'd just remembered the last straw. "Oh, Lord, Rocky, as bad as things are, why did you have to tell Clive we were engaged? Now I'm going to have to explain my way out of it, and the last thing I need is another complication."

Shrugging, he realized that he had no idea why the words had popped out of his mouth. He was not normally given to impulses—about one per decade was his usual rate. "I don't know, it just seemed like a good idea at the time. You'll have to admit, I'm probably safer than a Doberman."

She gave him a withering look. "Now, that I seriously doubt. By now Clive will already have been on the phone to my father. R.C. will have gained access to your F.B.I. file, checked out your voting record, your blood type, your bank balance, plus any outstanding traffic tickets."

"So? Is that a problem?" His life was an open

book. The few chapters not for public consumption, he had already ripped out and burned.

"Not for me—at least not after I explain that you were just—just—"

"Tilting at windmills?"

With a distracted sigh, she turned back to the window. In the clear morning light she looked both older and younger than he knew her to be. The shadows were back—those haunting, taunting shadows that he'd found so oddly intriguing the first time he'd ever met her.

Time to back off, he told himself. He'd done what he'd come to do; the next move was hers. "So what are you trying to say? That it's all over between us? You're giving me back my ring?"

If he'd hoped to erase that glittery look, he seemed to have succeeded. She swatted his arm with a handful of paper napkins. "What ring? The closest thing to a ring you ever gave me was offering to put phone jacks all over my house."

"That's me, Roland Waters, known on three continents as the world's biggest cheapskate."

"*Roland?*"

"You wanna make something of it?"

She bit her lip. The brittleness faded, but he wasn't fooled. She was still terribly fragile. So he said gently, "Hey, you can still use me if you think it'll help—or you can just go home, tell the truth and face the consequences. You're not your daddy's little girl any longer." Nor the wife of that jerk Sullivan.

"Which truth?"

Right. Which truth. He had a feeling it was far more than their phony engagement. "It's your call, Sarah.

If you don't want to face it right now, then don't. But, listen—you've got friends.''

She only looked at him, those large haunting eyes peeling layers off his heart like a pair of lasers. He wanted to hold her, but this was not the time. The lady was stronger than she gave herself credit for being, but to make that strength work for her, she had to trust it.

"Sarah, it might not always seem that way, but the world's a pretty terrific place—even Washington, in spite of what you read in the papers or hear on the nightly news. We both know what makes the headlines, but headlines aren't the whole story. Sometimes they're not even part of it. Honey, the world's mostly filled with decent people trying to live decent lives. Trying to create a little happiness for the people they love. You happened to get tangled up with a few of the exceptions, but that's just it—they're the exception, not the rule.''

Spoken like a blind optimist. Which he wasn't, never had been—never would be. Odd, the way she had of making him act out of character.

She stared at him as if he'd lost his last marble. "Well. That was...inspiring. Is the sermon over?''

Rocky shrugged and tried not to look embarrassed. "Yeah, it's over. Now you know why I gave up writing.''

"Pollyanna the journalist. Oh, my, you do have a problem.'' Sarah actually chuckled, and then, without thinking, she walked right up to where he stood massaging the muscles at the back of his neck and wrapped her arms around his waist. She knew precisely what her own problem was—make that plural.

She wasn't at all sure of his. So she just held him, sighing a little because despite her recent attempts at writing, she wasn't as good with words as he was, and anyway, it was going to take more than words to make things work out this time.

"Thanks for trying. It was a noble effort." And then, after several moments of utter stillness, she said, "I ran away, you know. I didn't know what else to do."

He nodded. At least she thought he nodded. He had a nice solid frame overlaid with a resilient layer of muscle that invited burrowing. And so she burrowed, pressing her face into that delicious hollow between chest and shoulder. "I didn't know how to fight back—or even who to fight. Running seemed the only logical choice. Is that what you did?" *After your Julie died,* she wanted to add, but couldn't quite find the courage.

The barriers were down. Rocky heard himself saying, "The first few years after the accident—once I finally accepted that Julie wasn't ever coming back—I took every assignment I could land. I'm not sure if it was running or hiding. Maybe both. But by the time I realized that the doctors were right—that she…that she wasn't aware—" He swallowed hard. "By that time I needed the money, too, so it wasn't only running away. It was—hell, I don't know."

"Staying busy helps. Wearing yourself out so you won't wake up at four in the morning and lie awake, wondering how much worse things could possibly get. Wondering why, just when you thought things were beginning to turn around, they…" She swallowed audibly. When she couldn't continue, he finished for her.

"They tanked. Got so much worse you actually toyed with the idea of surrendering. Four in the morning is a pretty vulnerable time for anyone. There's a physiological reason for it, only I can't think of what it is at the moment. I guess the practical solution is never to sleep alone. Then, if you wake up and see your whole life sliding downhill—"

"You'll have someone handy to apply the brakes. Did you ever think of writing a self-help column?"

He began to chuckle, causing sensations to race through her body that were indescribable, inappropriate and hardly helpful under the circumstances.

She disengaged and touched her hair, feeling as if she'd just been thoroughly kissed. Wishing she had. "For heaven's sake, I haven't even had breakfast and here it is past lunchtime."

"Hey, you've forgotten my *huevos rancheros* already? Lady, that's a low blow."

"Food doesn't count when you're stressed out."

He let her get away with it, knowing it was the quickest way out of a tricky situation. What he needed to do was make things easy for her and then step back and let her handle it. He had contacts in the medical world—hackers, if he couldn't get answers the legitimate way. She needed reassurance that the old coot wasn't about to pop off the mortal coil, needed to find out what Meadows was up to and set him straight once and for all. And then she needed some direction. Vegetating here in the country, while it might be pleasant, wasn't enough for an intelligent woman with a creative imagination.

But that was her call, not his. "You want to talk to your father and get his take on the situation?"

The look she gave him held a glimmer of the old Sarah Mariah—young, outnumbered but feisty as hell. "Now what makes you think he'd level with me? He never has before."

"I could find out for you how serious this heart thing is."

"You have access to confidential files?" She poked her head around the refrigerator door, then emerged with a jar of homemade preserves. "Watermelon rind. The last of Aunt Emma's stock. Well, do you?"

"Sure. I actually have a few legitimate sources, too, but if it will give you a thrill, we'll go underground first."

"Hand me the peanut butter. I guess it doesn't really matter, I'll have to go back, anyway. Lord, I dread it!"

Rocky handed her the jar from the cabinet, then took it when she was done with it. He got out a clean spoon, scooped out a big blob of extra crunchy and proceeded to eat it like a lollypop. "Will you stay?"

"With Father? Oh, Lord, no, I'd suffocate. But there's this birthday thing coming up, too. Whatever the situation is, I'll probably have to stay for that. He'd hardly be having a party, would he? I mean if he has a serious health problem?"

The rest of the day was spent getting ready to leave. Rocky hauled off the pile of vines and evergreen branches and dumped them into an irrigation ditch. By the time it could cause a problem with drainage, he'd be long gone. He fastened up a sagging gutter and cleaned out the pine straw, and while he was at it he swept off her roof. The thought of Sarah clambering around on the steep slopes was enough to cause him a few problems with his own heart.

How could a woman who moved with such regal grace, whose hand gestures might have been choreographed for butterflies—how the devil could she trip over her own feet? It wasn't her eyesight, he was pretty sure of that. Could the truth be as simple as she'd stated? That her mind was usually on other things instead of what she was supposed to be doing?

If she'd been an artistic type, he might buy it, but she was… Yeah, well—she was what she was. Sarah Mariah Jones Sullivan, daughter of a certified reprobate, widow of another one, and great-niece of Aunty Em. If he hadn't seen the name in the tax records, he might have thought she'd made it up—it was too much in keeping with their very first conversation.

Standing on the steep roof with a broom in his hand, Rocky surveyed the countryside. From that vantage point he could see seven buildings—houses, barns, sheds. Acres of woodlands, more acres of corn. A strip of blacktop and even, in the distance, a glimmer of water that was probably the Currituck Sound.

Cornfields and Aunty Em or not, this sure wasn't Kansas, but judging by the way she was attacking housecleaning, Sarah might have been leaving for Oz. Rugs were hung on the line. Sheets were laundered. Periodically she appeared on either the front or the back porch to shake out a rug or a dust mop.

There was something both satisfying and disturbing in the amount of work that got done before dark that day. For some people physical exertion was a means of escape—for others, a means of focusing the mind. In Sara's case, it might be a bit of both.

Rocky insisted on driving to the nearest barbecue place, a matter of several miles, and bringing back supper while Sara showered and packed her suitcase. He drove her car and filled the tank. Noticed it would need inspecting before the end of the month and made a mental note to remind her. The last thing she needed was another hassle.

He opened his laptop and caught up on his e-mail, deleting most of it without a second thought. Sarah wandered over, munching on a cold French fry, and watched. "I'm surprised you don't have one of these," he said. "Living so far off the beaten track, it's pretty handy to be able to check in now and then, read a variety of newspapers, see what's going on in the rest of the world."

"I'm sure it is."

"Sorry. Merely an observation, not meant to be taken personally."

"Bull."

"You want to try for an early start tomorrow?" They were skirting over some pretty thin ice. Neither of them mentioned the fact that she was about to beard the lion in his den. Or the fact that a man with all the scruples of a starving alley cat—with the help of his lawyer—was up to something that involved her.

Or the fact that once they parted, whether or not she returned to Snowden, there would be no reason for them to meet again.

"The sooner I leave, the sooner I'll be back," she said as if shoring up her resolve.

She was standing behind his left shoulder, frowning at the screen. His hands, too large for the small keyboard but agile from years of practice, rested on his thighs. "My offer stands," he said quietly.

"To go with me?" She shook her head and moved away, touching one polished surface after another, almost as if she were saying goodbye. "No, thanks. This is something I have to do by myself."

He nodded, knowing—sensing—she was waiting for him to argue. And dammit, he wanted to, but she was right. She needed to face down the enemy and walk away the victor—victress—whatever.

Sarah couldn't sleep. She was so tired she should have been able to lose consciousness instantly and sleep for a week, but her mind refused to shut down. It wasn't like that little computer of Rocky's—something, incidentally, that she was going to have to learn how to use if she was serious about writing. No matter how many times she hit the sleep switch, her mind wouldn't go blank. She continued to lie there, eyes open in the darkness, trying desperately to envision the next few days: "Hi, Father, you're looking well for a man who's supposed to be desperately ill."

He would say something gruff, turn away and pour himself a drink, whether or not he already had one. The senator wasn't a heavy drinker. Whisky, like his cigars—like his daughter—was a prop.

"I thought I'd drop by and wish you a happy birthday on my way to—"

He would see though it in a minute.

Rocky, dammit, I don't want to do this alone!

But she would, because she had to. Because until she dealt with the past, she couldn't begin to deal with the future. And the more she thought about it, the more determined she was that one way or another her future was going to include Kitty. Who else did she have? What were her chances of ever having a child of her own?

Rocky set his watch for six and settled down, knowing he wouldn't be able to sleep. He could do without for about twenty-eight hours before his judgment began to suffer. A few years ago he could have lasted at least forty. Fortunately, most of his other faculties were still intact. His libido, for instance.

His hearing was another. Sometime later he was just easing into the first stages of sleep when he heard a noise. A thud—something breaking...

Opening his eyes, he stared into the darkness, wondering if he'd dreamed it.

"Oh, damn, oh, damn, oh, damn, oh, blast!"

Adrenaline racing through his system, he was at her door within seconds. Waiting only for his eyes to adjust to the darkness, he called softly, "Sarah, are you all right?"

"No, dammit, I'm not all right! Go away!"

"Sorry—not an option."

"Then watch out for the broken glass, it's everywhere."

Ten

___

Without asking, Rocky switched on the overhead light. Sarah was sprawled on the floor beside the bed, her nightgown up about her hips, with one foot tangled in the bed linens. Near her outstretched hand were the remains of a broken glass.

"Don't laugh. Don't you dare say a word," she seethed. Reaching back, she tugged her nightgown down over her bare bottom.

Once his heart settled back in place and he assured himself that she wasn't seriously hurt, he said, "Don't move until I pick up the glass."

The scene told the story. She'd tossed off the covers, gone to the bathroom to get a glass of water, all without turning on a light, and tripped over the sheet on her way back to bed.

"I feel so...so stupid," she muttered.

"Yeah, it takes a really stupid woman to sprawl facedown when her foot gets tangled in a bedsheet." Kneeling beside her, he helped her turn onto her side, then scanned the length of visible flesh to be sure she wasn't bleeding anywhere.

"I'm all right—stop looking at me! At least I had sense enough to land on the rug."

"Nice planning. Next time aim for the mattress."

She whacked him on the shoulder as he lifted her from the floor and swung her over onto the bed. "Turn off that overhead light on your way out, will you?"

"Let me collect the glass first. You don't want to step on it when you get up in the morning." He was trying not to grin openly, knowing how defensive she could be when she was embarrassed. "The rug's wet—I'll roll it up and take it outside."

It was a white crocheted rug. Several slivers of glass sparkled on its nubby surface. Sarah, brushing off the soles of her feet, wondered if she could be genetically flawed. Her mother had never been clumsy. As for the senator, he'd always been surrounded by a coterie of aides who would have caught him if he even looked as if he was about to stumble.

Watching Rocky pick up broken glass, drop it in the wastebasket and then carefully roll up her bedside rug, her thoughts strayed from genetics to anatomy. Wearing only a pair of navy briefs, he reminded her of a Rodin sculpture. Gazing at the sweep of his back, the curve of his—

Yes, well…never mind.

Holding the carefully folded rug, he switched on the bedside lamp, put the rug outside in the hall, doused the overhead light and turned back toward her bed.

She followed his every move. There was no way she could help herself, he was such an alien presence in the room. He might even be the first man ever to set foot in the room that had once belonged to her maiden aunt.

Swallowing a sudden thickness in her throat, she lifted her eyes to his. And there it was again—that odd electricity, sharp as lightning in a summer squall, and just as hot.

Drawing her feet up before her, she wrapped her arms around her knees, creating a barrier that was no barrier at all when what she wanted so desperately was to break through every conceivable wall, including the wall of common sense.

"You still want a drink of water? I'll get another glass from the kitchen." The words were ordinary enough, but his voice sounded oddly strained.

"No, I want—"

He waited, his pale-gray eyes looking not at all cool in the light of a forty-watt bulb. Her gaze fell from his face to his chest and strayed down to the dark elastic band of his briefs.

She closed her eyes.

"Then I guess I'd better leave you to get some sleep," he said, and she shook her head.

"No, please—could you just—stay?"

He was visibly aroused, and obviously embarrassed about it. Sarah tried and failed to think of some graceful way to handle the explosive situation. In the world in which she'd grown up, plain speaking was a rarity. How did a lady gracefully tell a gentleman that she wanted him to take off his briefs, tear off her gown and make wild, passionate love to her without saying a word until neither of them had the strength to move?

"Sarah?"

"Please?" She opened her arms and reached up and quickly discovered that no words were needed.

The old mattress sagged under the added weight, toppling her against his side. She thought he might have said something under his breath, but by that time she couldn't have spoken if her life depended on it. Carefully he shifted her and resettled himself until they were lying side by side in the middle of the old-fashioned double bed. The sound of a shuddering indrawn breath broke the silence. His or hers—or both?

What are you waiting for? she wanted to cry. Just—do it! Pretend I'm someone you want—someone beautiful!

There was nothing in the least seductive about her nightgown. The most that could be said of it was that if her house caught on fire in the middle of the night and she had to run for her life, it wouldn't be terribly embarrassing.

What now? She'd made the first move; the next was up to him. If he wasn't going to do anything, then she might as well crawl under the covers and hide until he had the decency to leave.

The silence continued, loud as a ticking time bomb. *Coward! If you let him get away now, you'll regret it for the rest of your life!* Finally, eyes shut tight, jaw clenched, she said, "Would you—could we please make love?"

Moments later—it felt more like hours—Rocky said quietly, "Sarah, I'm not sure that's a good idea."

Then what are you doing in my bed? she wanted to ask. "Why not? Have you taken a vow of celibacy?"

You insensitive fool, his wife died less than a year ago!

The unspoken words hung there between them. She cringed, half expecting him to get up and walk away. She wouldn't blame him if he did. Finally he said, "No."

"I'm truly sorry, I had no right to ask. You can go now." Her eyes were still closed, as if by not seeing she could deny her part in the whole pathetic scene. "None of this is really happening, you know—you're only dreaming it. Tomorrow you'll wake up and we'll both get into our separate cars and leave. You'll probably drive south—maybe down to Oregon Inlet—you might even go fishing. Or maybe climb a lighthouse or something—there are lots of those around here. And after a while you'll wonder, what was that crazy dream I had a few nights ago all about, anyway? I'd better stop eating before I go to bed."

"Sarah?"

"You can never tell what brings on crazy dreams. Now me, I always dream really scary stuff when I eat pickles before bedtime. Pickled onions are the worst."

"Sarah?"

"I think it must be some crazy chemical reaction. Like batteries? You know, acid and—"

Rolling over onto his side, he took her face in his hands and kissed her.

Pity, she told herself. Oh, God, please not that!

But it didn't feel like pity. In fact it felt carnal from the first touch. In silent surrender, she wrapped her arms around his shoulders, her hands slipping on his sleek, warm flesh.

There were things she needed to say, but this was not the time. His hands moved down her throat to cup her shoulders and then they were on her breasts, his touch light as he gently cradled them in his palms. Against the heat of his palms, her nipples hardened almost painfully. Kiss me there, she pleaded silently, and as if he'd heard her wordless command, he moved lower.

Her gown was too much like a straitjacket. With his mouth tugging at her nipple, she reached down and grabbed a handful of the flimsy stuff, tugging it up as far as it would go. This was not the way it was supposed to work. In books, in movies, the heroine never got twisted up in her nightgown.

In books and movies, the heroine never had to beg. The hero would somehow manage to tear her gown down the front and it would fall from her shoulders, leaving him in silent awe of her newly revealed loveliness.

The trouble with reality was that nylon was tougher than duct tape and there was no graceful way to get naked without stopping the action.

Reality was when Rocky lifted her hips and eased the gown up a few more inches, and by twisting and wriggling she was able to work herself free. Reality was pulling the blasted thing over her head and having it catch under her chin.

Once freed, she reached toward his waist, but before she could do it for him, he removed his own briefs. Briefs were easier than full-length nightgowns. Feeling the satiny heat of him brush against her thigh, she nearly lost her nerve. You'd think she was a virgin, the way she was behaving, and she wasn't. She most certainly was not.

Even so, he was probably more experienced than she was. Her first affair had lasted only a matter of weeks until her lover had landed a job on the West Coast. She had always wondered if her father could have had a hand in his sudden departure. After that, there'd been no one until Stan.

But never before—not with her first lover, not even with Stan—had she felt such a fierce compulsion. Stan used to complain that her mind was never on what they were doing. But then, Stan had never been sensitive to her needs, her wishes, and after a while he'd been right.

This time she couldn't think of anything but her own need—the hot, heavy weight of her own desire. She was going to explode the instant he touched her, and his hand was inching closer, his palm on her belly, his fingertips brushing the slope of her mound.

Hurry, hurry, she wanted to cry—I need you now!

"Sarah—" His voice sounded as if he were choking on a bone. "I don't have anything to protect you. Do you happen to have—?"

She groaned audibly. "I don't care! Please?"

Fleetingly, she thought about the ways in which a single moment of pleasure could affect so many lives, but then he was moving even lower, kissing her where his hand had been, and then...

It took only a single touch—a single kiss. She shook with the explosive force of release—cried out as wave after wave of exquisite pleasure washed over her.

Gasping for breath, she clutched his shoulders and waited for the earth to settle down again.

And when it eventually did, she closed her eyes in despair.

As wonderful as it was, it wasn't enough. She'd wanted him inside her—wanted him to feel the same thunder, the same bone-melting fires. The heat that could fuse two individuals into a single entity.

He held her as if she were infinitely precious, and she wanted to cry. For him, not for herself. Or maybe a little bit for herself, too, because no other man had ever done this for her before. No other man ever could.

She loved him. There was no longer any room for doubt. She wouldn't say the words aloud, because to do so might imply an obligation, and that would ruin everything.

Not that she hadn't considered what it would be like to have sex with an agreeable partner. A nameless, faceless partner. She'd been told in all those sophisticated articles in women's magazines that good sex was a woman's right. She was free, unattached and certainly old enough to know her own mind. There was no reason not to enjoy herself sexually, as long as she used discretion. It was, if anything, a declaration of independence.

The one thing she had failed to take into consideration was that she might find herself deeply—head over heels, as the saying went—in love with the man.

So much for independence.

He made a trip to the bathroom, returned and slipped into bed again. Settling her against him, her back to his front this time, he wrapped his arm around her waist and whispered, "Go to sleep, Sarah—the alarm's set for six."

Certain she would never be able to sleep feeling so guilty and embarrassed, Sarah had closed her eyes. Hours later when she awoke, she was lying on her back. She stared up at the ceiling as incredibly detailed memories washed over her. It was like falling asleep and waking up in a brand-new world.

A sound from across the room broke the fragile process and she turned her head. "Rocky? What are you doing?"

He was seated at her desk, wearing yesterday's jeans and khaki shirt, his feet bare, a frown on his freshly shaven face. "You want to tell me about this?" He indicated the stack of manuscript and drawings.

Sarah closed her eyes again. It wasn't enough that she'd given him her body—now he wanted to claim her secrets? Her dreams?

"Dabbling," she said with a sigh, wishing there was some dignified way she could get out of bed and pretend last night had never happened. The story, she could deal with—there was nothing at all to tie it to Kitty.

The other—the unilateral sex—that was something else. She'd fallen apart in his hands and given him nothing at all in return.

"Would you mind?" she said, looking pointedly at the door. "I need to get showered and dressed if I'm going to get out of here anytime soon."

The trouble with morning light was that it was utterly merciless. Her hair was a mess, she had already discovered places where his beard had scraped her skin. She didn't want to think about how her face must look.

Her nightgown was folded neatly on a chair on the other side of the bedroom. Fine. Great! Then she'd wrap herself in the damned bedspread!

And trip on it? her inner voice jeered. Way to go, Sarah. You're a real class act.

Eleven

They might have been strangers for all the words spoken between them as they ate a hasty breakfast and cleaned up afterward. "Is one bag all you're taking?" he asked politely, checking the back door to be sure it was locked.

"That and my purse. I won't be gone long."

He gave her a searching look, but said nothing. How odd, she thought, that the event that had brought him here—the release of a book rehashing the scandals surrounding her late husband, seemed irrelevant now. There had been no more reporters since the first flurry.

"Ready?" He held the front door for her.

There were so many questions she wanted to ask about what had happened between them last night. With bitter amusement it occurred to her that she didn't even know how to frame the first question, even if she could have brought herself to voice it.

He'd been right to call a halt, of course—if that's what had happened. If Stan had been as responsible—or if he'd been a faithful husband in the first place, then she'd probably have still been living in Arlington. There would have been no Kitty. By now she might even have been pregnant with a child of her own.

"I topped off your tank yesterday," Rocky said as he put her overnighter in the back seat. "If you weren't so stubborn about getting a cell phone—"

"I know, I know." She shaded her eyes against the glare of the sky. "Look, I'm getting there, all right? I'm going to buy a computer and learn how to use it, and then maybe I'll try a cell phone, but don't rush me."

Actually, she had one. Stan had tried to show her how to use his home computer. He'd laughed when she hadn't been interested and told her to come out of the dark ages, that practically every kid in America was hooked up to the Internet. She was the only woman in Washington—possibly in the entire world—who didn't have e-mail. He'd tried to talk her into getting a cell phone and a pocket pager—he'd even mentioned some gadget she could carry in her car that could tell her where in the world she was at any given moment in time.

"I know where I am. That's what street maps are for," she'd told him. It had done no good to explain that she'd been far too accessible all her life. "There's such a thing as privacy, you know. I happen to value mine."

But Stan had loved gadgets—the more expensive, the better—almost as much as he'd loved the lime-light. He'd insisted on giving her a phone that plugged into her car's cigarette lighter. The thing had never worked properly, and she'd never bothered to tell him or to find out why. It was somewhere in the trunk of her car, along with her tire-changing tools—which she *did* know how to use, if she had to.

Rocky looked angry and frustrated. She knew how he felt, having seen the same look on both Stan's face and her father's when she didn't instantly bow to their superior male knowledge.

"Look, I'll be all right, don't worry," she exclaimed. "Believe it or not, people were safely crossing continents before cell phones and global positioning gizmos were even invented." He was standing beside his car, which looked as though it had been driven a few thousand miles past its use-by date.

"Sure." He looked as if he'd like to say more. Instead, he climbed in under the wheel, closed the door and rolled down the window. "Stick with the writing, Sarah. Judging by the few pages I saw, you're good. And by the way, your left rear tire is wearing. You need to have your wheels balanced."

Sarah closed her eyes and prayed for patience. "Would you please give me credit for possessing a brain? I'll balance my own damned tires! That is, I'll—"

He was grinning. The righteous, meddlesome, wonderful, generous man was grinning!

"Oh, for gosh sakes," she muttered as she climbed into her car, tossing her purse on the passenger seat on top of her sunglasses, a candy bar and an envelope she couldn't recall seeing before. Probably an old shopping list.

She really should have called her father to let him

know she was on her way. If he was truly ill, she needed to know it. In that case she would stay with him until she could find someone—maybe a practical nurse—to live in. It would cost a fortune, and she didn't know if he still had insurance or not.

She would simply have to deal with the situation as she found it. If he wasn't really ill—if he was bluffing, something at which he was a master—then she might or might not stay for his birthday. It would depend on how much he gloated.

In either case, the sooner she saw him, the sooner she'd be able to find out the truth, satisfy her conscience and get back to Snowden.

Ever the dutiful daughter, she thought bitterly.

"Ever the doormat," she amended as she braked to avoid a suicidal squirrel.

When Rocky had asked her over breakfast about the drawings and manuscript on her desk, she'd told him it was a hobby—that she hadn't quite made up her mind whether to write children's stories or a survival guide. If he'd made the obvious remark—that anyone less qualified to write a survival handbook would be hard to find—she might have broken down and told him everything.

But he hadn't, and so she'd left it at that. After that, conversation had been practically nonexistent. They'd both been eager to leave. Besides which, she hadn't been able to look at him without thinking—without remembering—

And dammit, he'd known it!

Glancing in her rearview mirror, she swore again. If he thought for a single minute she was going to put up with being followed all the way to Maryland, he was in for a surprise. She might be technologically challenged, but she was a damned good driver.

She tried and failed to lose him on the 64 bypass around Norfolk. Once on the Eastern Shore, she took several detours, whipping suddenly off the highway onto narrow roads, passing farms and the few remaining fishing communities before looping back to the highway. By the time she stopped for a late lunch near Salisbury, he was nowhere in sight. Which should have made her feel triumphant.

Instead, she felt depressed.

Well, what did you expect? It's over, okay?

Not okay. Whatever had happened between them, it had ended with no real harm done on either side, she told herself. But she didn't have to like it.

Her crabcake sandwich suddenly lost its appeal. Finishing her iced tea, she dug out a tip, glanced through the plate glass window to be sure there was no slightly rusty, slightly battered, dark-green SUV among the half-dozen vehicles in the graveled parking lot.

Hearts don't actually break, she rationalized, it only felt that way. She had brought it on herself—this miserable, empty feeling—by falling in love with a stranger. A man she had known for little more than a week.

Plus twenty-odd years, technically, but that didn't count.

Back in her car she slung her purse on the other seat. The envelope slid off onto the floor. She leaned across and picked it up, felt something small and heavy, and curious, traced the shape with her fingers. A key?

Even more curious, she turned the envelope over. Someone had scribbled an address and phone number on the back. Now why in the world would anyone give her a key? What was she supposed to unlock?

There was no message, no note, only the phone number, and a street address in Chevy Chase.

"Damn you," she whispered. "If you think all you have to do is whistle and I'll come running—"

That very first day he had stood in the middle of her dusty, weed-grown lane and whistled. The piercing sound had slowed down the reporter—the first reporter—long enough for Rocky to catch up with him.

And she'd looked at him—at those icy eyes, that square, unshaven jaw, and something had happened to her. Whatever it was—hypnosis, airborne virus or a major tectonic-plate shift, it had obviously affected her brain, hormones, her judgment and totally destroyed any sense of self-preservation she might once have possessed.

The rambling rock-and-redwood house was large, but hardly palatial. The land itself was probably more valuable than the house, which had been built back in the seventies. A dozen or so acres, most of it in its natural state, on the banks of the Wye River. The shell driveway was edged with daylilies that had become naturalized over the years. Tall trees were just beginning to show a touch of fall color. It really was a lovely place, Sarah admitted as she drove slowly past the house and parked in front of the three-car garage. By all rights she should have been happy to live here. She'd been invited to do so after Stan had died, except that would have meant being constantly at odds with the senator, whose ideas concerning women and children had been set in concrete before she'd been born.

As a child, he'd used her for photo ops, but he'd never made the least attempt to get to know her. As a woman, he had chosen her associates, discreetly getting rid of a few of her closest friends, not that she'd realized at the time why they had suddenly cooled off or moved away or started seeing someone else. He had even engineered, she'd realized belatedly, her marriage to a promising young congressman.

Now that she was widowed, he would no doubt expect to oversee her social life, possibly even to the extent of marrying her off again to a suitable candidate. She had an awful feeling that this time that candidate might be Clive Meadows.

"When hell freezes over," she muttered as a weathered, middle-aged man came around the corner of the garage, rake in hand. Ollie had been with her father for years in one capacity or another. The senator was good to the handful of people he trusted.

"Hi, Ollie. How's Annamarie?" The handyman's daughter was in her third year at Annapolis.

"Hurt her shoulder playing soccer, Miss Sarah." He had called her Miss Sarah ever since he'd come to work for her father some twenty-five years ago. "She's doing real good, though. Smart as her mama was, God bless her."

"I know she is, Ollie. Will I be blocking anyone if I leave my car here for now?"

"Leave the keys in 'er, I'll shift 'er if I need to." Ollie came from a long line of Chesapeake Bay watermen. Cars, like boats, were of the feminine gender.

"The senator's out back on the patio with Mr. Mead-ows."

She was tempted to tell him to leave the engine running in case she needed to make a quick getaway. Instead, taking the flagstone path around the house, she told herself that the sooner she found out what was going on, the sooner she could cope with the problem and leave with a clear conscience.

Later, lying awake in the guest room she had used only a few times since her father had bought the property back in the eighties, she thought over the past few hours and tried to decide what it was all about—why she'd been summoned.

According to the senator he'd recently had a small scare, not that a man his age didn't expect such things. Simple angina, nothing to worry about...*this* time, he'd told her. She'd recognized the stoic martyr role. He'd gone on to tell her that he took pills for his blood pressure, which was a tad high. As for his cholesterol, he ate like a damned rabbit and took pills for that, as well. One bay of the three-car garage had been turned into a torture chamber where he was supposed to sweat out the rest of his days on a bunch of confounded machines.

"What do the damned medics expect from a man my age? Clive, get me my cigar."

"Father, you probably shouldn't—"

He silenced her with the same peremptory gesture he'd used whenever she'd tried to tell him something as a child. "I've cut down to two a day. Might as well die if I have to give up everything that makes life worth living." He cackled, and that, Sarah thought, was the most telling sign that he was pushing eighty. He could no longer manage the hearty laugh that had once been so much a part of his image—not without coughing.

She knew very well there was something more—something he wasn't telling her. J. Abernathy Jones had always been skilled at telling a partial truth and seamlessly blending it with lies. She'd do better trying to get the unvarnished truth out of that old willow stump down by the pier.

With Clive for companionship, plus R.C., Ollie and the woman who came in a few hours each day to do the cooking and minor housekeeping, her father really didn't need her. Any filial obligation she might have felt had ended when he'd let her go through the ordeal with Stan alone. Oh, he'd returned in time for the funeral, but that, she suspected, was more because it gave him an opportunity to play his favorite role before the photographers waiting outside the cemetery than out of any real concern for his daughter.

Exhausted, she finally fell into a deep sleep. Hours later she awoke when leaf-dappled sunlight fell across her face, feeling surprisingly refreshed. No wonder people often sought a change of scenery after a trauma. Distance really did help. Added perspective, at the very least. Hadn't she discovered as much when she'd cut all her ties and moved to Snowden?

Two days later she was no closer to discovering what it was that her father wanted from her. The three of them, she, Clive and the senator, had quietly celebrated his seventy-ninth birthday with a dinner of broiled fish with lime, baked potato with fat-free sour cream, a large salad with an olive oil dressing and an apple cake for dessert. J. Abernathy had complained bitterly as he scraped the last bite from his plate.

Sarah had to admit that he looked far better than he had the last time she'd seen him. Obviously, the new restricted regime agreed with him physically, even if it didn't do much for his state of mind.

"I'll be leaving tomorrow, Father." They had dined on a glass-topped table out on the back patio, with the hum of a distant outboard, a thousand tree frogs and the hypnotic sound of a bug zapper filling the silence.

"Surprised you stayed long's you did. I might be an old man, but you're not getting any younger, either, daughter."

"I'd noticed," she said dryly.

"It's still not too late." He cast a sly look at Clive, who was testing the flexibility of a new fly rod.

Reluctantly, Sarah took the bait, knowing that the sooner she put an end to whatever plans he might have up his sleeve, the sooner she could get away. "I'm afraid to ask...too late for what?"

"Legacy. Yes sir, a man my age, who's accomplished all I have, he needs himself a legacy. I'd like to think there'll be another generation coming along behind me to carry on."

Clive coughed discreetly. Sarah's mouth fell open.

His *legacy?* All he had *accomplished?*

The man had disgraced himself personally, lied under oath and endangered national security, for starters. His trial alone had cost the taxpayers millions, not including all the wasted hours involved. The press had been merciless and to her sorrow, Sarah knew he'd deserved every scathing headline.

"Is that what Stan was supposed to do—carry on your legacy?"

The senator dismissed the question with an expressive snort. "Sullivan was a lightweight. I thought the boy had possibilities, but turns out I was wrong." His shoulders slumped and he sighed. "I reckon I owe you an apology, daughter."

"That's not necessary. We were both—"

As if she hadn't spoken, the senator continued to speak. "If that baby of his had been a boy, we might've managed to salvage something."

Sarah caught her breath. *That baby of his?*

"Didn't think I knew about that, did you?" The old man's eyes took on a wicked gleam. "Not much goes on I don't know about, missy. It might pay you to remember that before you go shacking up with every Tom, Dick and Harry that comes along."

"Every Tom, Dick and...?" But of course he knew about Rocky. R.C would have told him, which was why and he'd sent Clive down to investigate. Dammit, couldn't she have a single thing for herself? "Father, please stay out of my private life. Believe it or not, I'm perfectly capable of choosing my own friends."

"Damned reporter. Nosy bunch of hyenas."

Not that he hadn't used them for his own ends over much of his public life, she thought with bitter amusement.

Clive, who'd been an unobtrusive bystander all this time, poured an ounce of brandy in a glass and placed it in the palsied hand. "One more won't hurt you, I guess. Want to try out that new fly rod tomorrow evening, just before dark?"

But Sarah wasn't about to be distracted. ''Father, how did you know about—about Kitty?''

''How d'you think I knew? Damned leaches went to Clive when they couldn't get hold of me—it was right in the middle of all the mess. Told him if I didn't pay off they'd go public about Sullivan's brat. Said the girl was underage when he got her in trouble— said they could get DNA if they had to, but there'd been plenty of witnesses, more than enough to make the charges stick.''

If a sigh could be said to express piety, his did. ''Said to myself, more scandal's the last thing that little girl of mine needs, so I paid 'em off and told 'em if they knew what was good for 'em, they'd take the money and shut up.''

Sarah felt sick.

Clive wandered over to the edge of the patio and stared out at the fireflies floating over the overgrown tangle of mock orange, spirea and wigelia. The senator drained his glass and traced the ring of moisture on the table with a thick forefinger.

''You knew about Kitty all along?'' Her father frowned. Clive looked embarrassed. ''Father, these people are no better than blackmailers. I've been paying them, too.''

Her father nodded. It occurred to her then that he'd known all along about that, too. No wonder she suddenly felt as if a noose was tightening around her throat.

''Figured you'd be worried about the little nit. All that work you did with those poor kids. Good work, too,'' he added hastily, noticing her expression. ''Admire you for it, always did. Noblesse oblige, and all that crap.''

Sarah stood, her jaw set in a way that would have served as a warning if he'd ever bothered to get to know her. "You don't even know the meaning of the word," she said grimly.

"Now, Sarah—"

"I want that child, Father. I'm not about to let her grow up with people who use her for blackmail, even if they are her own grandparents. They can't love her—they'll neglect her and possibly worse.''

"Well now, that's what I thought you might say. Sit down, girl. Why don't we have another drink and talk about it, you, me and Clive, here? Did I mention they'd sent a picture of the br—the little girl?''

Later Sarah sat cross-legged on the bed and stared down at the snapshot of a child who had been fathered by a man she had once loved enough to marry. A man who might have given her a child of her own. In the picture Kitty was wearing a diaper and a pair of red tennis shoes. She should be out of diapers by now. Her hair was cottony white. There was dirt on her little face, and in one hand she held a doll with only one arm. Were those tear tracks down her cheeks?

Sarah's arms curved instinctively as if to embrace a small child and then fell back to her lap again. She was only a baby—babies cried over the least little thing. It didn't necessarily mean she was unhappy, or being mistreated.

But the Poughs—Kitty's own grandparents—had used that tiny innocent to line their pockets. According to Clive they had actually offered to sell her if the price was right. And of course Clive had known Sarah could never have come up with the money. He'd been the executor of her mother's will. He had handled Sarah's small trust fund and evidently poked his fingers into more of her financial affairs that he was legally entitled to do.

Sarah had pried the whole story from them. Neither man had wanted to talk about it at first, but she'd insisted. It was the first time she remembered ever winning in a tug-of-war with her father. She still wasn't certain which one of them had come out victorious, because the battle was still not over as far as Kitty was concerned.

Trust J. Abernathy Jones to come up with a convoluted scheme that would pay off his best friend for past favors, tie his daughter to him forever and, incidentally, salve his own conscience by making up for years of paternal neglect. Kitty was to have been the bait. Both men knew Sarah had been making monthly payments—they had known almost from the first. And knowing Sarah and the work she'd done, first as a senator's daughter, then as a congressman's wife, for underprivileged children, they had known precisely where to apply pressure.

She might even have agreed to stay on without the added inducement if her father's health had been precarious, but no way in hell would she ever have agreed to marry another of his handpicked candidates. Especially knowing they would stoop to using a child as bait.

Clive had recently undergone treatment for prostate cancer. He was in the wait-and-see stage now. He'd resigned from the lobbying firm and had recently suffered some severe financial reversals.

Oh, they'd worked out the perfect plan, Sarah told herself bitterly. Two old friends, once powerful, now sinking into obscurity together, sharing a house on which, incidentally, Clive had paid off the mortgage, back in the days when a friend in high places had come in handy.

Here, they were close enough to the political action to watch from the sidelines while they worked on their respective memoirs. Meanwhile, the dutiful daughter of one could look after them both.

What an enormous debt her father must owe the man. Evidently Clive knew where all the bodies were buried, so to speak. No longer able to attract, much less afford, younger wives, he faced spending his declining years either alone or with a cantankerous old widower.

Which was where Sarah came in. As her father had said, what else did she have to do, for God's sake? It wasn't as if she had a husband or a career. All she had to go back to was an empty, run-down house in the middle of a damned cornfield.

Knowing how Sarah had always hated being an only child, and how she'd spent almost her entire adult life working in some capacity with children—having heard all about a woman's biological clock—they had come up with the perfect plan.

No wonder Clive had come back for a second attempt at prying her loose after meeting Rocky. It had never occurred to either of them that there might be another man in her life. She wasn't beautiful, she wasn't wealthy, she'd been publicly humiliated. Except for her volunteer work, she'd never even been particularly outgoing. Socially she was barely adequate.

But then, their socializing days were largely over, so that hadn't been a consideration.

Neither man cared for children, although the senator had certainly kissed enough babies to get himself elected and reelected over and over, both to the House and then the Senate. But that was a sacrifice they were prepared to make.

Somewhere in another room, a clock struck eleven. Sitting cross-legged on her bed, Sarah continued to hold the photograph of the child she had pictured so differently. She'd given her Stan's face, his light brown hair. Whatever he'd been on the inside, the man had been physically flawless.

There was nothing at all familiar about that small, dirty face staring at the camera, and yet...

Kitty would be almost two years old. She shouldn't still be wearing diapers at that age. Someone could have washed her face before they took her picture, at the very least.

"Poor darling, you don't deserve any of this," Sarah whispered.

How many organizations had she helped raise money for that fed poor children worldwide? How many drives had she organized to help fund child health care and set up free walk-in clinics in poor neighborhoods? How many hours had she spent at children's hospitals, reading stories, listening to their shy confidences? Feeling their tiny hands creep into her own?

She had to do something about this child. Clive was

a lawyer, but if she asked for his help she'd end up caught in the clever trap they had devised.

Oh, they had known her weakness, all right. And under the gentlemanly patina, both men were equally without scruples when it came to getting what they wanted. And what they wanted now was a strong, healthy woman who would feel morally obligated to stay here and look after them in their declining years, regardless of any sacrifice it might entail on her part.

Sarah had learned last night that two cooks and three housekeepers had either quit or been fired. Annie had stayed on as long as she had for Sarah's sake, despite J. Abernathy's despotic ways. In a time of nearly full employment and high wages, it was a wonder Ollie and R.C. were still here. The senator must have promised to remember them in his will.

Clive had moved in during the course of his treatment. Which was only logical, as he was a part owner. The reason his beach house had been conveniently empty was that he'd put it up for sale, along with his town house on O Street.

Sarah gazed down at the snapshot again and felt the trap begin to close. It was far too easy to visualize a towheaded little girl running around the backyard, chasing butterflies, fishing from the pier, catching the school bus when she was a little older.

Once, briefly, she had dreamed about another child, the first of several, visiting a kinder, gentler grandfather....

It hadn't happened. Now it never would. Was it so very selfish of her to want this one child for herself? In the early months of her marriage, she'd had such dreams. Later, Stan had always said. After the next campaign, after the election. But even then things had begun to change between them. As a naive young bride, she'd been thrilled at the privilege of standing behind her statesman husband while he helped pass laws to right the nation's wrongs. As a wife, she had quickly learned to fill her daytime hours with volunteer work, attend the requisite social functions and lower her own expectations. After all, although he was her husband, he'd been sent to Washington to work for his constituents, for his country, not to play house with his bride.

How could she have been so naive, having grown up around politicians? Mariah Jones had quickly come to terms with her husband's demanding profession. She had become one of Washington's favorite hostesses and, as busy as she'd been, she had still found time to be a wonderful mother. "Get your head out of the clouds, child," Sarah could remember hearing her say more than once. "If you don't stop stargazing, one of these days you're going to walk into a tree and break your neck."

Instead, she'd broken her heart.

But hearts were resilient, and here was a child who needed someone to love her. That, Sarah told herself, she could do.

That she was *determined* to do.

Rising abruptly, she crossed to the dresser and felt inside her tote bag. It was still there—the envelope with the key. The more she thought about it, the more she was beginning to have bad feelings about Kitty's situation. If the Poughs had contacted her father, asking for money, too, then they didn't deserve this child.

She would deal with her father's health problems

later if she had to, but first she had to know the truth
about Kitty's situation. If she was secure and happy
where she was, then that would be that. Right or
wrong, Sarah would go on sending money as long as
she could afford it. Perhaps someday she might even
find a way to be a part of the child's life. She could
be to Kitty what Aunt Emma had been to her.

Aunt Sarah Mariah. She rather liked the sound of
that—but first she had to discover the truth of the situation, and there was only one man she knew of who
could help her do that.

Twelve

With the game being played out on television—
eighth inning, score tied, two out, three on base for
Atlanta, Rocky paced the floor, returning again and
again to the window overlooking the street. Traffic
was light. The view of the small parking area was
blocked by the tops of two ginko trees and a weeping
cherry. She could be out there right now, trying to
make up her mind whether or not to come in, and he
wouldn't know it. What if she made it all the way to
his door, then lost her courage and fled?

He should never have allowed her to face that conniving old pirate alone. Whatever else he was, the man
still was her father, and a woman like Sarah, with her
queen-size sense of responsibility, would never be able
to walk away if he managed to convince her that he
needed her. She had stuck by his side throughout the

hearings, her very presence giving mute testimony to the fact that he couldn't possibly be as wicked as he'd been portrayed, despite the damning evidence. A few years later she'd been thrown to the lions all over again.

But no more, dammit. He had allowed her to go in alone because it was something she had to do for herself if she ever hoped to be free of the man. After a year of living alone in Snowden, she'd still been afraid to answer the phone. He'd seen animals cower in their pens long after the gate was opened. Prisoners who huddled in their cell after years of confinement, unable to comprehend that they could simply walk out. Not answering her telephone wouldn't cut it. Sarah had to confront the man and then walk away unaided to be truly free. And she had to do it alone.

Rocky had halfway expected her the second night. Not the first, because knowing Sarah, she would give her father enough time to fully present his case. When she hadn't shown up, he'd called her number in Snowden and let it ring twelve times. That didn't necessarily mean she wasn't there. Sarah had a habit of not picking up. As far as she was concerned, the telephone was a one-way instrument, and that one way led out, not in.

Rocky shook his head in reluctant admiration. The lady might not look it, but in some ways she was as tough as that damned grapevine she'd been fighting all summer.

Sarah, Sarah, where the devil are you? One more day and I'm coming after you.

What was that old song about not having time to

play the waiting game? Sometimes it seemed as if he'd spent half his life playing the waiting game.

Suddenly Sarah couldn't wait a single moment longer. Arriving in the middle of the night meant she'd have a harder time finding the address, but if she waited until morning he might be gone. He might still be in North Carolina, for all she knew. Rescuing some other woman in distress. "Oh, stop it! It's going to be bad enough without imagining the worst!"

She had told her father at supper that she was leaving, knowing he'd assume she was going back to Snowden. Lying by omission. She hadn't lived with two politicians as long as she had without learning how the game was played. "I need to think it over, Father. I'll call in a day or so."

"We could fix up a room. One kid—how much trouble could she be? Get her some swings, slides—whatever you think she needs."

When had he ever concerned himself with what any child needed? "I'll call," she'd repeated. Then, for the first time in years, she had kissed him.

Back in her room she'd fretted herself sick, wondering if she had the right—if she even had the courage to ask for Rocky's help.

It wasn't just an excuse to see him again—at least, not entirely. He had resources—he would know how to go about handling something this delicate. The investigations, the personal negotiations, the legal aspects. Twice she picked up the phone, only to put it down again. If she called first, what could she say? *I want you to forget what happened between us and help me adopt a baby?* He'd think she had lost her mind.

It was nearly ten when she left. Her father had gone to bed early, and Clive was on the phone. Sarah felt no compunction at all in leaving without saying goodbye to him, although she couldn't help feeling a certain degree of admiration. His own career had risen and fallen along with that of his friend. Such loyalty, if that's what it was, was probably a rarity in their world of shifting alliances. She'd like to think they both deserved such loyalty.

Her car was still where she'd left it when she'd arrived. R.C. came by every morning. The housekeeper came for a few hours each afternoon. Other than that, no one but the mailman had been in or out. Driving slowly down the winding driveway, she had to admit it was a lovely place. Maybe someday she would come for a longer visit.

And bring Kitty?

One step at a time, she warned herself. And the next step would be a giant one.

Near the 301 exit, she stopped for gas, coffee and a bathroom. Pausing for a lull in the traffic, she toyed with the idea of turning south instead of continuing to the beltway. After her botched attempt to seduce him, Rocky was probably glad to have escaped with his virtue more or less intact.

On the other hand, he'd given her the key. Why would he have done that unless he expected her to use it?

Face it, Sarah. You've got the survival instincts of a lemming.

But dammit, she loved the man and she needed him, and whatever he thought of her—whether or not he could ever learn to love her back, she was pretty sure he would help her with Kitty because that was the kind of man he was. Decent, honorable, caring.

Against the eerie glow of the streetlights, the sky was pitch-black, adding further fuel to her doubts. It wasn't too late to turn back. She could be in Snowden by suppertime.

No, dammit, this was her decision and she would follow through, no matter what. If he wasn't there, she would let herself in, use his bathroom, maybe raid his refrigerator…he owed her that much…leave his key and maybe a note, thanking him for—

Well, whatever. He could interpret it any way he wished.

With the help of a detailed map, she finally located the street, then crept along until she found the right address. After parking illegally under a huge ginko tree, she sat for several minutes, going over in her mind what she would say if he happened to be there: Hi, I was in the neighborhood, and I thought I'd drop by.

Glancing at her watch, she wondered if she was crazy even to think about adopting a child, especially under the circumstances. She certainly didn't owe it to her husband.

What did she know about being a mother? Looking back, she realized now that quality time for her own mother had been a few minutes each morning to let her daughter know her day's schedule. "I'll be at the museum until one. You can reach me through the front office." Or, "I'll be at the fashion show until four— I'll try to bring you a scarf, or maybe one of those darling little berets."

Quality time for her father was whenever he was

slated to appear in public. His wife and daughter had been bit players, of slightly less importance than his speechwriter and his hairdresser. They represented living proof of what a worthy statesman J. Abernathy Jones really was. Defender of home, family and the American way of life.

"Bull," Sarah growled. Leaving her overnight case on the back seat—not a particularly smart thing to do, but she was too tired to be clever—she locked her car and headed toward the front entrance.

Tonight's game had gone to twelve innings. Rocky had slept through the final one. Fallen asleep in his chair. Then he'd got up and prowled in the kitchen, making a pot of coffee, scrambling the last two eggs in the carton. He was going to have to make a supply run soon, but he'd been afraid to go out, afraid of missing her.

He ate standing up, knowing he'd probably doze again if he got too comfortable. On the other hand, if he went to bed, he'd never be able to sleep.

Hell of a thing, not knowing. He should never have let her go without some sort of an understanding. And now one more night had passed. One more day of waiting and wondering. How long should he give her? Three days? A week?

Hell no. He'd give her until noon. If she'd decided to stay with her father, she could just damn well *un*-decide. At least until he'd had a shot at changing her mind.

He had tried working on a column. Ideology, how it affected issues, and how it could be distorted for public consumption. About twelve hundred words in, he gave up.... Sarah, Sarah, don't waste what we could have together.

At first when the buzzer sounded, he couldn't think what it was. He glanced at the phone, scowled at his watch and when it hit him that it was the buzzer in the lobby, his first impulse was to go down and let her in personally. But if he was going to disgrace himself with a maudlin display of emotion, he'd as soon do it in the privacy of his own apartment.

What if it wasn't Sarah?

It was Sarah. He knew it in his bones. And if she thought for a single minute he was going to allow her to walk out of here without a commitment, she'd better think again.

He was waiting in the hallway when she reached the top of the stairs. Neither of them spoke, but it was all there. Whatever it was between them that had brought her here, that had made him so certain she would come.

There were shadows under her eyes. Her various cowlicks had defeated any attempt she might have made to groom her hair. And she was so damned beautiful he could have wept.

Rocky opened his arms, and she walked into them without a word. Long moments passed before she lifted her face from his shoulder. "I probably should have called first."

"No need to. If you hadn't showed up by noon I'd have come after you." Pulling her with him, he backed toward his door and closed it behind them.

"Where? Snowden or my father's house?"

"Hadn't made up my mind yet. I'd have followed

my instincts and found you, though, you can bet on it.''

He was still holding her, swaying gently from side to side, his eyes closed to better absorb her essence. *She's here. She's actually here in my home, here in my arms.*

After so many anxious, sleepless hours, all he could think of was taking her to bed. If he did nothing more than hold her until she was rested, it would be enough.

The hell it would. At his age, mind over body should be no problem, but with Sarah, all bets were off.

''Are you uh—hungry?'' he asked, easing her away before she realized what was happening to him. The last thing he wanted was to scare her off now.

''I had coffee. I would have had peanuts, too, but I spilled them in the car trying to open the pack.''

His laughter broke the tension. ''Why am I not surprised?''

He led her into his living room, noticing for the first time the lack of anything more than the basic furnishings. When it had become obvious that Julie would never be coming home again, he had moved from the town house they'd shared. Moved several times, in fact, as financial necessity dictated, paring his possessions down in the process. When it came to creature comforts, a man didn't need much more than the basics.

''You look bushed.''

''I haven't been sleeping well,'' she admitted.

Nodding, he continued to embrace her with his eyes. She was actually here, within touching distance. ''Would you like, uh—''

"I could use a bathroom," she said with that funny half smile he had come to look for. Come to love.

"Through here. Give me your car keys and I'll bring in your bag. Then we'll have supper—breakfast—whatever, while we talk."

She hesitated just a fraction too long.

"Sarah, you can prioritize any way you want to, but we're going to talk, we need to eat, and I have a feeling we could both use a few hours of sleep."

Lifting her hands, she raked her fingers through the layers of her thick brown hair. "If I could just splash some cold water on my face. Actually, all over would be better. I had to drive with the window open to stay awake, and I probably reek of exhaust fumes. There was a tanker ahead of me practically the whole way."

She didn't look grungy, she looked windblown. Exhausted. Irresistible. "Sure. Meanwhile, I'll see if I can scrounge up something to eat. Or I could send out."

"I'm not really hungry. Coffee would help, though, because the talking's going to take a while. There's something I want to ask, but first there's something I need to explain."

Rocky nodded. He had a feeling he was about to get to the heart of the matter. "Go shower while I put the pot on. Then we'll talk."

If he could keep his mind on what she was saying instead of what he'd really like to do. Suddenly he wasn't feeling quite so tired. Instincts grown dull from lack of use told him it wasn't about the Cudahy book. That had been launched a week ago, making a much smaller splash than the publisher had hoped, thanks to new offerings by a couple of perennial bestsellers.

"Give me your car keys, I'll get your bag while you wash up."

Some ten minutes later Sarah stepped out of the shower and wrapped herself in a lush, king-size bath towel. Whatever he might lack in decorative accessories, she thought with amusement, the man didn't stint on luxurious necessities.

Hearing movement just across the hall, she cracked the door and called out, "Rocky? Would you mind looking in my bag for my wrapper? It's the blue-flowered thing."

Clutching the towel more tightly around her, she tried to remember whether or not she had packed anything of an embarrassingly personal nature when she'd tossed everything into her overnighter. *He's seen you naked, you ninny! The sight of your underwear is hardly going to bring on cardiac arrest!*

When he rapped on the door, she opened it a few inches and reached for the cotton wrapper "What's that cliché?" she asked breathlessly. "'We've got to stop meeting like this'?"

"You mean, déjà vu all over again? I didn't know you were a baseball fan."

The sound of his husky murmur sent ripples along every nerve in her body. With his face mere inches away, Sarah struggled against a strange sense of lethargy. Heat pooled in the lower regions of her body, robbing her of the will to move—to think. "I...I—I'd better..." Tearing her eyes from his face, she stared down at the wisp of cotton in her hand. She meant to say, "I'd better put this on—make myself decent," but somehow the words wouldn't come.

Soap-scented steam drifted through the door, enclosing them both in a seductive cloud. Rocky reached for her hand. She dropped the duster he'd just handed her, clutched at the towel, and he said, "You don't need your robe, Sarah. We've got some unfinished business, remember?"

Wordlessly, she nodded, her gaze never leaving his face. His meaning was perfectly clear. This time there would be no halfway measures, no unilateral completion. This time they would make love in every sense of the word. Later they would have to talk, because she needed him for Kitty's sake.

But right now she needed him even more desperately for her own.

The bedroom was as uncluttered as the rest of the apartment. Bed, chest of drawers, chair. No pictures on the wall. No clothes tossed casually over a chair. The room reflected the man. Private. Self-contained. Understated. An easy man to love, but not an easy man to get to know.

Sarah perched on the bed, and he pressed her back against the pillow. Then slowly, deliberately, his eyes never leaving hers, he peeled her fingers from the damp towel she wore like a sarong and spread the ends apart. Feeling heat envelop her body, she hoped he would think she was still flushed from the hot shower.

His eyes never left hers, and Sarah wondered how she could ever have thought gray eyes were icy. Still wearing a rumpled white shirt open at the neck and a pair of khakis, he smelled of laundry soap and warm, clean male. She told herself that anyone who could bottle and sell the scent as an aphrodisiac would make a fortune.

"Wait. I have to tell you something first," she said,

suddenly feeling the urge to put all her cards on the table. She was sick of subterfuge.

His gaze moved slowly past the hollow at the base of her throat, lingered on her breasts, then on her navel before moving on. She wondered how merely looking, not even touching, could generate so much heat.

"I'm listening."

"Well. What it is—that is, I'm pretty sure I love you. I…I wasn't quite certain before."

She heard the sharp intake of his breath. "Mind telling me what decided you?"

"Now? Do I have to?" When he nodded, his features frozen in a stern mask, she looked away and whispered, "It just…came to me. And I wanted you to know before we—that is, I wanted you to know in case you wanted to back out."

With a softly muttered oath, he lowered himself across her body and began kissing her as if he were starved for the taste of her mouth.

Eventually Sarah's greedy hands found their way inside his shirt. When a finger brushed over his nipple, she felt him stiffen. Somehow, without breaking away from his mouth, she managed to free him of the shirt, and then they both went to work on his pants. Two pairs of hands fumbling desperately, driven by a desire so fierce it blocked out the rest of the world.

"Lady, you don't pull any punches, do you?" He groaned and closed his eyes.

Once she had freed him of his outer garments, Sarah gazed down over his splendid torso, and she said shakily, "I didn't mean to upset you." With one finger, she traced a path through the pelt of dark hair that embraced his male nipples, then led down to his waist and beyond.

The physical response was fierce and immediate. Breathing through his mouth in short, rapid gasps, he fought for control. "This is absurd in a man my age," he muttered.

Sarah—a shy, inhibited woman who had been called frigid more than once by her own husband, could only agree. "Me, too."

Who *was* this wanton creature? This teasing, taunting woman who actually laughed aloud as she pushed him over onto his back and sprawled across his body. Moving her hand slowly over his large body, she began a leisurely exploration of all the exquisite textures—the velvet and satin—the fur and hot steel.

"Whoa—hold on a minute, love," he whispered. Lifting her aside, he sat up and opened the drawer of his bedside table. Her eyes widened as she caught a glimpse of the contents. Catching her look, he said, "First stop I made after leaving my door key in your car, I stocked up. Is that blind faith, or what?"

"Oh, my. Maybe we should have talked first, after all," she whispered eagerly. "We might not have time—" And then she slapped a hand over her mouth.

Chuckling, Rocky said, "Later, I promise. First let's put out a few wildfires. Otherwise neither of us is going to be able to concentrate."

Moments later he lifted her hand to his lips and traced the fine lines across her palm with the tip of his tongue, savoring the sharp intake of her breath. Then, his gaze never leaving her face, he closed his mouth over the tip of one finger and suckled gently. By the time he was finished with the first five, she was lying on her back, clutching his thigh and whimpering.

By the time he finished saluting the last finger with a heated, moist caress, Rocky was close to the whimpering stage, himself, but he was determined that this time they would share the glory.

"Now? Please?" she whispered.

Seeing the feverish glitter in her eyes, knowing it was reflected in his own, he moved over her. How was it possible that a woman he had known less than a month—a month plus some twenty-odd years—could affect him so powerfully, in so many different ways?

They came together then, and his last glimmer of reason was eclipsed by a surge of white-hot heat.

Again they came together...and then again. Eventually they fell asleep in a sated tangle of limbs.

Rocky awoke to the sound of kitchen noises. Moments later, the events of the past few hours slipped neatly into place in his orderly mind, and he marveled that such a thing could happen twice in a man's lifetime.

It was more than sex, as mind-boggling as that had been. More than simple release. There had been no one in years who had meant anything to him other than momentary physical release. Even that had brought such feelings of guilt he'd finally accepted his celibate fate.

They'd probably been too young, he and Julie, but they'd loved as only the very young can love. Idealistically, with the future spread out before them, they had lain awake at night after making love, planning for the future—sharing dreams.

For months after the accident, his whole world had narrowed down to that one small room in a private hospital. He had watched her lying there day after day, week after week. Waiting for some sign. Gradually hope faded, replaced by anger at the senselessness of it all. And then slowly, even his anger had faded, replaced by a love that had deepened in ways he couldn't begin to comprehend. It would always be a part of him though—that love—tucked away in a safe place in his heart.

And now there was Sarah. His sweet, awkward Sarah with the earnest eyes and the funny half smile. Sarah, who had been the innocent victim of two men who should have loved her more.

Rocky was on his way to the bathroom when he heard the sound of breaking glass from the kitchen, followed by a soft, "Oh, damn, oh, damn, oh, damn."

Grinning, he stepped into the shower and turned on the water, full force. By the time he had shaved and dressed in jeans and his favorite black knit shirt, he was whistling. All of seven minutes had passed. Record time, and he hadn't even nicked his chin with the razor.

"I smell coffee," he said, pausing in the kitchen door. He managed to resist the urge to sweep her into his arms and carry her back to bed, but there was no way he could dislodge the smile on his face.

"I broke one of your plates. The green one. I'm sorry, but it was ugly, anyway. How can anyone make breakfast from bread, bottled tea, salsa and hot banana peppers?"

"What, you don't like fake pizza for breakfast?"

Over a makeshift breakfast, they talked. Sarah sprinkled sugar on her toast, Rocky spread his with salsa and peppers. Then she carefully placed her crust on her plate and faced him across the table. "All right," she declared, grimly earnest. "Here's what you have to know before you can help me—that is, advise me."

He let her run with it. Whatever secret she'd been guarding, she'd get it out in her own sweet time, in her own way. One thing he'd learned about Sarah— she was no pushover.

"You know about Stan—I mean, all that mess he was involved in. Some of it was illegal, most of it was just...messy. It all came out only because there were some celebrities involved, and somebody broke out a window and started throwing things out. Furniture. A neighbor reported it and a reporter heard about it on his car radio and...well, I guess you know all that. What you don't know—nobody does, because they don't publicize that kind of thing—is that at least one of the girls involved was underage."

He waited. In her own time, in her own way, she would get to the heart of the matter. He poured her another cup of coffee, sweetened it with one spoonful of sugar and added a splash of half-and-half.

"Well. The thing is, she had a baby. This girl, I mean. And she claimed it was Stan's."

"And you believed her?"

"Stan confessed. He told me he didn't realize how young she was, not that that makes it all right. The thing is, there's this child—hardly more than a baby— and her name is Kitty, and her mother doesn't want her, and her grandparents are getting money for her and—"

"Getting money from where? How? Sarah, don't

tell me you're being blackmailed.'' What possible difference could it make to her now, he wondered, if
another of her late husband's sins came home to roost?

Small fists clenched on the table, she leaned forward. ''They're her grandparents. They're old—living
on social security in a trailer somewhere in Virginia
Beach. The mother married and she's gone—I'm not
even sure if they know where she is. But this much I
do know—that baby deserves someone to love her,
and anyone who demands money just to protect her
from vicious gossip can't. Love her, I mean.''

He waited. He had a feeling he knew where this
was headed, but she needed to get it all out.

''They contacted my father, too, and he gave them
money because he didn't think I needed to have all
that mess come out again. And it would—especially
with that awful woman's book. I can just imagine the
headlines.''

''Tabloids, maybe. No reputable newspaper would
touch it.''

''So? People read tabloids. I always read them while
I'm waiting in line at the grocery store. Not that I
believe them, but some people might, and Kitty
doesn't deserves to grow up under the shadow of all
that mess. Children can be cruel unless someone
teaches them to be kind. Maybe it's part of the survival
of the species thing, I don't know. I only know,'' she
said with a sigh, ''that a child needs to be loved for
who she is, not used.''

He didn't say a word. There was a wealth of understanding in those clear gray eyes of his, but she
didn't dare trust too soon. She waited for him to tell
her she was crazy—that it was none of her business.

That nothing could change what her husband had done.

Instead, he said quietly. "You want the child, am I reading you correctly?"

Sarah took a deep breath and closed her eyes. Then she nodded. "Yes, but there's more. You might as well hear it all."

So she told him about the plan her father and Clive Meadows had concocted between them to get her to move in and take over the reins so that neither of them would have to be bothered with petty domestic issues. "They don't have a clue—there's always been someone to do for them. Annie was with my parents since they were first married. R.C. said the last three housekeepers walked out, and the one they have now is a retired dietician who doesn't do floors, windows or much of anything but cook, send out the laundry and make the beds."

He could picture her managing her father's household like a feisty little general. But it wasn't going to happen. Not if he could prevent it.

"So now you see why I'm so determined to adopt that baby."

Setting his brain on fast forward, Rocky wondered if he had missed a vital clue. "Because you don't want to move in and take care of your father."

"Because Kitty needs me a lot more than my father does. And because I need her. And obviously they don't. The Poughs, I mean. And Kitty's mother. So why shouldn't she go to someone who will love her and take good care of her?"

"What if her mother decides she wants her back?"

Sarah frowned. "What if she doesn't?"

"Can you afford a child?"

"I can't afford not to try. She needs me."

It was as simple as that, Rocky told himself later, after he had agreed to help her explore the possibilities. Which would mean finding out the price, putting it in terms that could be done legally, locating the daughter and getting her to sign off.... It would take some tricky negotiating.

They both fell silent. Sarah picked up grains of sugar with her fingertip and thoughtfully licked them off. Rocky watched, wondering if he was crazy to be thinking of starting all over again at his age.

Well, hell...he'd never know without asking. "Sarah, you know about Julie. You know I'm currently unemployed. I have a few investments, a few royalties, but Julie's long illness maxed out my insurance and wiped out all our savings. What I'm trying to say is that I'm no bargain. Living alone for so long, I've picked up a few bad habits that I might be too old to change, but I'm willing to try."

"What are you trying to say?"

"This is not about Kitty, this is about us." Eyes shouldn't be that large, he thought. Nor that direct, that expressive. "A kid needs family—brothers and sisters. You didn't have any—I didn't have any. Julie came from a large family, but they're all on the West Coast and all a lot older. She used to call herself the afterthought."

He wasn't sure she was making the connection. Maybe he'd lost his skill with words, so he opted for plain talk. "You've got to know I love you. It's the only way I can explain a normally sensible guy behaving in such an irrational manner."

Seeing the look in her eyes, he had to wonder which she was questioning—the sensible part or the irrational part. "Like heading out on a rescue mission uninvited. Moving in with a woman I barely knew. Hanging shutters, for God's sake. You've had me tied up in so many knots, wondering if I was crazy to think—to hope—"

"Go back."

"Back?"

"Back to the beginning."

Mentally he backtracked through what he'd just said. "You mean the part where I said I love you?"

Beaming, she nodded. "Say it again."

So he did. And then she did, too. And hours later as they lay in bed, bare feet entwined, and discussed the possibilities, the words were spoken more than once in the silent language of lovers.

There were obstacles to be overcome—there would always be obstacles. But together they could deal with whatever the future brought. The healing time was over, the building time just begun.

Epilogue

———

"**H**urry up, honey, Grandaddy will be here before you know it." Sarah waited while Kitty gathered up the toys she wanted to show her gruff, overindulgent grandfather. It was more than two small arms could carry, so Sarah took the big panda and the sock monkey.

"My book, Mommy, don't forget my book!"

"Don't you dare," Rocky warned, appearing in the doorway just as Sarah braced herself to squat and retrieve the book from the bottom shelf. Getting down, she had discovered, was no problem. It was getting up again, with her balance distorted by her seven-month pregnancy, that caused problems.

"I thought you were finishing up your column?"

"Proofing it. Figured I'd better see what my ladies were up to." He handed her the well-worn book and kissed the tip of her nose. It was Sarah's first published book, with the second one of the series almost finished. Kitty loved spelling out her own name in the dedication.

"I'm hardly breakable, you know," she said dryly to the husband who insisted on treating her as if she were made of spun glass.

He didn't have to say a word, all he had to do was raise his eyebrows.

"Oh, all right, but once Roland is born, I'm not going to let you coddle me this way."

"Right. After little Mariah is born, it's back to bungee jumping, motorcycle racing and skateboarding."

Laughing, Sarah swatted him on the arm as they followed Kitty to the front door. With his past, he would probably always be a bit overprotective. And after the constraints required of a politician's family, she was still exploring the parameters of her own independence. Secure in their love, they were both mature enough to work through any conflict.

"I see G'andaddy and Unca Clibe!" Kitty shouted. Wriggling free of Rocky's restraining hand, she raced outside, spilling toys down the front hallway. The screen door slammed shut behind her just as a car pulled up in front of the house.

On the front porch Rocky wrapped his arms around his wife's expanding waist and waited as two old reprobates he had learned to enjoy, if not to respect, braced themselves for Kitty's exuberant greeting.

"Remember," Sarah said softly, "no talking politics."

"I won't if you won't," Rocky said, his smile a wicked taunt. He loved sparring with her, and had even come to enjoy taking on her father and his crony. "Remarkable, isn't it, the way a couple of old guys who don't particularly like kids manage to spoil ours the way they do."

"They're just practicing up on Kitty. Wait'll they meet Roland."

"Mariah."

"Patience, love—we'll get around to using both names in due time."

With a private little smile meant solely for him, she murmured, "I'm game if you are." Then, with the smile she had honed for public consumption as the senator's daughter and the congressman's wife, she said, "Hello, Father—Clive. Come on inside, supper's almost ready."

*   *   *   *   *

THE FORTUNES OF TEXAS

invite you to meet

THE LOST HEIRS

Silhouette Desire's scintillating
new miniseries, featuring the beloved

FORTUNES OF TEXAS

and six of your favorite authors.

A Most Desirable M.D.—June 2001
by Anne Marie Winston (SD #1371)

The Pregnant Heiress—July 2001
by Eileen Wilks (SD #1378)

Baby of Fortune—August 2001
by Shirley Rogers (SD #1384)

Fortune's Secret Daughter—September 2001
by Barbara McCauley (SD #1390)

Her Boss's Baby—October 2001
by Cathleen Galitz (SD #1396)

Did You Say Twins?!—December 2001
by Maureen Child (SD #1408)

And be sure to watch for *Gifts of Fortune*,
Silhouette's exciting new single title,
on sale November 2001

*Don't miss these unforgettable romances…
available at your favorite retail outlet.*

Where love comes alive™

CALL THE ONES YOU LOVE OVER THE HOLIDAYS!

Save $25 off future book purchases when you buy any four Harlequin® or Silhouette® books in October, November and December 2001,

PLUS

receive a phone card good for 15 minutes of long-distance calls to anyone you want in North America!

WHAT AN INCREDIBLE DEAL!

Just fill out this form and attach 4 proofs of purchase (cash register receipts) from October, November and December 2001 books, and Harlequin Books will send you a coupon booklet worth a total savings of $25 off future purchases of Harlequin® and Silhouette® books, AND a 15-minute phone card to call the ones you love, anywhere in North America.

Please send this form, along with your cash register receipts as proofs of purchase, to:
In the USA: Harlequin Books, P.O. Box 9057, Buffalo, NY 14269-9057
In Canada: Harlequin Books, P.O. Box 622, Fort Erie, Ontario L2A 5X3
Cash register receipts must be dated no later than December 31, 2001.
Limit of 1 coupon booklet and phone card per household.
Please allow 4-6 weeks for delivery.

**I accept your offer! Enclosed are 4 proofs of purchase.
Please send me my coupon booklet
and a 15-minute phone card:**

Name: _____

Address: _____ City: _____

State/Prov.: _____ Zip/Postal Code: _____

Account Number (if available): _____

097 KJB DAGL
PHQ4013

July 2001
COWBOY FANTASY
#1375 by Ann Major

August 2001
HARD TO FORGET
#1381 by Annette Broadrick

September 2001
THE MILLIONAIRE COMES HOME
#1387 by Mary Lynn Baxter

October 2001
THE TAMING OF JACKSON CADE
#1393 by BJ James
Men of Belle Terre

November 2001
ROCKY AND THE SENATOR'S
DAUGHTER
#1399 by Dixie Browning

December 2001
A COWBOY'S PROMISE
#1405 by Anne McAllister
Code of the West

MAN OF THE MONTH

For over ten years Silhouette Desire has been
where love comes alive, with our passionate,
provocative and powerful heroes. These ultimately,
sexy irresistible men will tempt you to turn every
page in the upcoming **MAN OF THE MONTH**
love stories, written by your favorite authors.

Available at your favorite retail outlet.

Silhouette®
Where love comes alive™